ATILUS THE LANISTA

Borgo Press Books by E. C. Tubb

Assignment New York: A Mike Lantry Classic Crime Novel
Enemy of the State: Fantastic Mystery Stories
Galactic Destiny: A Classic Science Fiction Tale
The Ming Vase and Other Science Fiction Stories
Mirror of the Night and Other Weird Tales
Only One Winner: Science Fiction Mystery Tales
Sands of Destiny: A Novel of the French Foreign Legion
Star Haven: A Science Fiction Tale
Tomorrow: Science Fiction Mystery Tales
The Wager: Science Fiction Mystery Tales
The Wonderful Day: Science Fiction Stories

THE ATILUS TRILOGY

1. *Atilus the Slave*
2. *Atilus the Gladiator*
3. *Atilus the Lanista*

ATILUS THE LANISTA

THE SAGA OF ATILUS, BOOK THREE: AN HISTORICAL NOVEL

E. C. TUBB

THE BORGO PRESS
MMXIII

ATILUS THE LANISTA

FIRST BORGO PRESS EDITION

Published by Wildside Press LLC
www.wildsidebooks.com

DEDICATION

For Annalise

CONTENTS

CHAPTER ONE

Streaming through the tinted glass set in the roof of the solarium, the morning sun threw patches of soft, multi-colored light over the chamber. Smears of red and orange, green, blue, pale violet, and amber dappled the floor, the furnishings, the figure of Aquilia Sabina in her stola of embroidered silk, and the man who stood respectfully before her.

"Domina." His bow was deferential. "It is an honor to attend one so gracious."

Praise that she ignored. "You have it?"

Again he bowed. He was a trader from Syria, smoothly plump with oiled and scented hair. His hands were heavy with gemmed rings and his robe was of the finest linen. Turning, he gestured to his slave and, lifting the lid of a long box the man carried, took out a sword. Offering it to the woman he said, "Here it is, Domina. Made in Damascus of the finest steel. The edge will cut through bronze."

She made no effort to touch it. "Atilus?"

I took the weapon and lifted it to catch the light. The polished surface of the blade shimmered, a glow that rippled as I moved the steel.

"Note the markings," said the trader. "The sure sign of a true, Damascened blade. One honed to perfection and hardened with countless blows. The edge is as sharp as a razor. The point also—rest it on your thumb and it will draw blood. I swear by the gods that no finer weapon was ever forged by the hand of man."

A table stood close against a wall; my belt and sword lay on it. Drawing my sword from its scabbard, I rapped the blade against the one the trader had brought. The metallic chime was as sweet as a bell.

Aquilia was impatient. "Do you like it?"

"A moment."

Again I tested the ring of the metal and then examined the balance of hilt and blade, turning to slash at the air, recovering to stab, to spring to one side, to thrust in a quick series of movements which sent their message into my hand and arm. The balance was perfect. The hilt fit my hand comfortably and, although it was gilded, it had none of the softness of gold. It was a good, workman-like tool, and I said so.

"My reputation is of the best," the trader said quietly. "I would not offer an inferior weapon to any man whose life depended on it. And surely, only the best is good enough for the most noted gladiator in Rome. The blade will hold its edge longer than most. It will shear through toughened leather and, as I have said, cut bronze. The finish is as you see. The price—" he hesitated, looking at the woman—"is modest."

The sword was good, but I had a sword, one I could trust. And it took more than an edge to cut through bronze or bone. Again I lifted the blade, prolonging my examination.

"There is, of course, a scabbard," said the trader quickly, reaching again into the box. "One worthy of the weapon."

More than worthy. It was heavy with gold, encrusted with jewels, the product of a master artist. Real, easily disposable wealth, which the sword was not. For the first time I smiled.

"A good blade," I admitted. "One I would like to use in the arena."

"And you shall." Aquilia settled the matter with a lift of her hand. "If you want it, Atilus, it is yours."

I sheathed the blade as, bowing, the merchant retired with his slave. A gift, but one I had earned, one I would have to continue to earn.

"Atilus." Now that we were alone, her voice became warm and soft. "Have I pleased you?"

"Always, Aquilia, you please me."

"And you don't think I'm a stupid old woman?"

To answer I lifted her hand and pressed it to my lips. Old she might be, but not that old, and certainly far from ugly. She could have given me ten years, but in the soft light no one could have guessed it. Tall, slim, hips and thighs smoothly curved, her breasts large and firm, she had a body many younger women would envy. Art had turned her hair into a mass of ebon; a startling contrast to the cultivated whiteness of her skin. Only when her cosmetics were washed away could the tiny mesh of lines around her eyes be seen. They, together with the fine tracery on her upper lip and the slight sagging of the skin beneath her chin, were the only signs of her advancing years. Minor flaws for which her generosity more than compensated.

And she had other attributes. In Rome a man was wise to choose his friends with care, especially a man who depended on his popularity. A gladiator had to stay in the public eye and be seen risking his life in the arena. Bedding rich women was an easier way of earning a living. It had been over a year now since I had last faced an opponent on the sand.

"I was speaking to Claudia Calvin the other day," she said. "She was curious about you, Atilus. She kept wanting to know how good a lover you were. Naturally, I said nothing."

"Is she rich?"

"Yes, but mean. You would be wasting your time with her."

"And with any woman other than yourself, Aquilia."

The flattery pleased her and she smiled, but she was a daughter of Rome, and as wise and as cynical as the culture which had created her. The culture of which I was becoming more and more a part. The blood price I had sworn to extract never seemed to be enough. To subject proud patrician women to the embraces of an ex-slave was a form of revenge. A revenge that I think Aquilia sensed and understood.

We had met soon after Verdalia had died, and in the following years she had taught me how best to use the money I had won. Now I needed no advice and, while still lovers, we had also become friends.

"Atilus!" Her hand rested on my hair. In the upper chamber her bed would be waiting, slaves discreetly absent should she decide to use it. Then, as I reached for her, she shuddered and lowered her hand. "No, my darling, as much as you tempt me, I must be firm. It would take too long for the maids to restore my beauty and we haven't the time. Already we should be at the Circus."

For days now all Rome had been in a ferment, the air filled with talk of nothing but chariots, teams, noted drivers, and the prospects of victory. Blood had been spilled in ugly battles between rival factions as wagers had risen and tempers grown short. Now, like the roar of distant surf, voices rose from the great amphitheater, the seats crammed with all who could beg, buy, or steal a ticket.

The ivory tokens Aquilia had obtained gained us entrance. The attendant smiled when he recognized me.

"Atilus! This is a pleasure. The last time you fought you won me a score of denarii."

"You should have sold your wife and backed me with what she would fetch."

"Sold her? I couldn't give her away." He frowned as he looked at the tokens. "These are in a bad position, Atilus. You won't get much of a view."

"Can you do better?" I slipped coins into his hand. "Something close to the finishing line and not too far from the podium?"

In Rome gold would buy anything, and we both were wise in the way things were done.

Settled, program in hand, I studied it as Aquilia made herself comfortable at my side. The races were numbered and each consisted of four teams, one from each stable. Each chariot was pulled by four horses harnessed abreast. Their names and colors were listed on the program together with details of their charioteers and the position from which they would start.

We'd arrived late and the first two races were over. Slaves were busy clearing away the debris of the last, among it a dead horse and the torn body of a man. The horse had a broken neck; the man, trapped by the reins that he'd wound around his waist, had been dragged from his chariot and trampled beneath the hoofs of a following team. A common occurrence, especially when, at the end of a race, each team strove to take the lead.

With nothing happening at the moment, there was time to look around.

The attendant had found us good seats close to the finishing line, on the second tier above the podium. We had a clear view of the stalls and were high enough to see a little beyond the Spine, which ran down the center of the amphitheater. It was built of stone and supported small altars and images of the gods. At each end was a column surmounted by a crosspiece. On one was set seven marble eggs, on the other an equal number of carved dolphins. One of each was taken down at the completion of every lap. A race was about four miles.

"Atilus! Look!" Aquilia dug her elbow into my side, her finger pointing to an entry on the program. "See?"

The fifth race and a name: Lucius Domitius Ahenobarbus. Nero's name.

"It must be a mistake."

"No." Her eyes told me she had secret knowledge. "It's no mistake."

"A joke then." I still found it hard to believe. Nero was an artist dedicated to the Muses, not a sweating charioteer. "A joke," I repeated. "A name used to cover another's identity. The Emperor would never take part in a race."

"But if you're wrong, Atilus?"

A chance to make some easy money. If Nero was racing, it was certain he'd be allowed to win. I rose and went in search of someone to take my wager. I didn't have to look far.

"A bet, Atilus? Certainly." Silannus Regulus produced his tablets. "On which race and for how much?"

"The third. Green for five gold pieces."

"Taken! And?"

"The fourth. Red for ten." As he made the notation I added casually, "And the fifth. Green for fifty."

Lowering his stylus, the man slowly shook his head. "No bets on the fifth, Atilus."

"Why not?"

"The omens are bad," he said blandly. "Last night a dead man came to me in a dream and held up five fingers, at the same time shaking his head. And this morning I tripped on the fifth stair. A man must pay attention to such omens."

"I don't believe in them."

"No?" He shrugged. "Well, I do, so no bets on the fifth."

Not with him and not with anyone in his trade. To try would be a waste of time, and the next race was about to begin.

"They're off!" Aquilia rose in her seat as the chariots raced from their stalls. "They're off!"

The cry was taken up and repeated by others until the air shook with the roar.

Tense in their flimsy vehicles, the charioteers made no acknowledgment to the crowd. Dressed in swaths of leather, hard round hats on their heads, their hands gripping the reins wrapped around their waists, they had thought only for their teams. Eyes wide, mouths open, the horses pounded over the sand. Trained beasts each worth the price of a hundred slaves.

The first curve was reached and taken without incident; one of the symbols resting on the crosspiece was taken down as they passed. Completing the lap, they came into sight again with Red in the lead, Green close behind, Blue and White at the rear racing wheel against wheel, swinging wide, and hoping to race ahead and cut in front of the others.

White, on the outside, saw his chance and took it. His inside wheel slipped behind the outer wheel of Blue and, as he swung out away from the Spine, the metal rim ripped into wood and tore the wheel from its axle.

Immediately the Blue chariot toppled, shattering into splinters, the driver snatching his knife and cutting the reins. He was fast and lucky. As his team raced on, dragging the ruined chariot behind it, he rolled free and ran to the safety of the stands.

At the fourth lap the others were running nose to tail, Red in the lead, Green in the middle. For two more laps they held that position and then, as they entered the last lap, White made his attempt. Again he tried to catch a wheel but Green was too clever for him. The chariot swung wide, bumped against the inside horse of the White, and broke its stride. It took the next-to-last turn and vanished beyond the central barrier.

Close to me a woman screamed, "Win, Orestes! Win and I'm yours!"

Orestes, the driver of the Green chariot, would be showered with similar offers if he managed to snatch victory.

Incredibly he did.

I heard the roar of the crowd, the screaming of women and men as, swinging out, he urged on his team. A burst of speed, expertly timed and maneuvered, sent him racing down the finishing stretch well in the lead.

"We've won, Atilus! We've won!"

Aquilia was on her feet, her face flushed, her eyes sparkling, every muscle in her body tense with excitement. An emotion reflected all around and one that would intensify as the day progressed. Worked into a mania, spectators would shriek and tear at their clothes, fondle each other, make ridiculous wagers, and even claw at their own skin.

From a vendor I bought wine and handed it to my companion. Sipping it, she calmed and resumed her seat.

"Aren't you going to collect our winnings?"

"They can wait. I know Silannus. He won't run away."

"What have we on the next race? Ten on Red?" She frowned at the program. "Diocoles, a good driver, but he starts from a bad stall. I'd back White."

"Even odds?"

"Yes. A hundred gold pieces. Taken?"

"Taken."

She had judged well. White made a good start, gained the inside, and held the lead for three laps. On the fourth, Red, taking a chance, forced the White chariot close to the three cones set at the foot of each end of the Spine in order to protect the stone. White, misjudging, veered too close and the inside wheel hit and lifted. In a flash, his chariot had overturned.

"Clocchis!" The crowd yelled the driver's name. "Clocchis!"

He couldn't hear them. Trapped by the reins, he was dragged after the horses, the overturned chariot slewing toward him, wood splintering, bright metal fittings strewn over the sand. I saw his hand snatch at his knife, the gleam of sunlight from the blade, and then it was over.

Diocoles, unable to avoid the wreckage, drove straight at it, hoping that the speed and skill of his team would pull him through. He almost made it, then the offside horse trod on Clocchis, stumbled, and pulled the other horses after him.

At once the sand was a mass of kicking, screaming beasts, smashed chariots. A red stain of blood stretched out behind the body of Clocchis as, crushed to a pulp, he was dragged over the sand. Diocoles, favored by the gods, had managed to cut his reins and lay against the stone as the other chariots thundered past.

As slaves rushed to clear away the wreckage, Aquilia slumped back into her seat.

"I've lost," she said. "Curse the luck. Atilus, you're the richer by a hundred gold pieces."

And the poorer by the ten I'd backed on Diocoles, but still the day showed a good profit. As the race ended I bought more wine.

In the tier before me a knight spoke thoughtfully to his companion as he studied his tablets.

"A private wager, Mercallus? On the second team in the next race to pass the finishing line. I've fifty pieces which says Ferdo will be the one."

"The Blue charioteer?"

"Yes. Is it a bet?"

Mercallus grunted, studying his program. Out of curiosity, I did the same.

Ferdo's inner horse was a Centenarius, one that had won over a hundred races, and would wear a specially adorned harness. The driver himself had a good reputation and was a favorite of the Blue faction, but his team consisted of Sicilian horses which, though fast, were unreliable. The necessity of slowing them to allow Nero to win would unsettle them—a fact which the knight had overlooked.

Leaning forward, I touched him on the shoulder.

"My pardon, but I overheard your conversation. If you would be interested in extending your wager, I would be grateful to be accommodated."

He was younger than I had thought, with a sharply delineated face and deep-set eyes of pale blue. They widened as, turning, he saw me.

"Atilus! This is a surprise. What brings you here?"

"A holiday."

"One which I hope will soon be over. You fight all too rarely these days. We miss you. It isn't kind of you to deny your supporters the spectacle of your skill." His eyes moved to the woman at my side. "Hello, Aquilia. I was telling Atilus that he is needed on the sand. Good sword-work is rare and a man shouldn't neglect his skills."

"I agree, Drusillius." Her hand closed with warm intimacy on my thigh. "Perhaps, if the offer was large enough, he would be interested."

"In a private display?" His eyes clouded with thought. "Perhaps it could be arranged. But, in the meantime, the bet. How much did you have in mind, Atilus?"

"A hundred pieces."

"That Blue will not come second." He made a note on his tablets. "And you, Mercallus?"

As he turned away Aquilia whispered. "A fortunate meeting, Atilus. Drusillius Augustus has wealth and influence. With him behind you, you could go far."

As far as my sword would take me. Drusillius was one of those who was more interested in a display of skill than the butchery the crowd demanded. Such skill was best appreciated at close hand, and that was the reason he'd mentioned a private bout. The spectators would be rich and, with such patrons, a successful gladiator could live like a prince. For as long as he could hold his own.

There was no mercy for the fallen and I was aware of it. The rooms beneath the amphitheaters were full of reminders: broken-down fighters who had been lucky to escape with their lives, victors too badly maimed ever to fight again, freedmen who had lost their nerve and had quit while they still had the chance. Cripples, men with missing limbs and empty sockets where once there had been eyes, those with faces pounded into nightmare masks, some who dragged themselves over the ground with calloused hands, their bodies useless below the waist. Victims never mentioned by those who lauded the games.

The trumpets sounded and the fifth race began.

CHAPTER TWO

The Circus Maximus was shaped like a long U, the flat end containing the processional gate and the starting stall for the chariots. As the trumpets sounded, the four teams dashed from their waiting positions. A gasp rose from the crowd as they saw the Green chariot. It was covered with gold and studded with gems; even the metal rims of the wheels were gilded and the extended axles, set with bands of gold, had knobs of silver. The horses were equally magnificent; their harness gilded, their manes braided with bright ribbons.

Nero himself matched the extravagant splendor of the display, dressed in leather, gilded and set with gems. The round hat on his head was a gleaming ball of gold, broken only by the tall, thick plume of horsehair dyed a bright green. Like Apollo himself, he caught and reflected the sun so that he moved in a glimmering nimbus of light.

His team, selected thoroughbreds from Libya noted for their staying power, raced into the lead and headed for the inner position. It was too great a lead and, normally, the judge would have declared a false start, but he was not a fool, and the rope stretched from the end of the Spine to where he sat was lowered long before Nero reached it.

Like a blazing thunderbolt, the golden chariot streaked down the track well ahead of the others.

As a display it was magnificent, but as a race it was a foregone conclusion. Even so, Nero handled his team well, cutting sharply around the curves, swaying back to tighten the reins lashed around his waist, leaning forward to give the animals their heads.

After him came the others. For them the second place would determine the real victor, and each did his best to gain it. As I'd guessed, the Blue team was unsettled by the drag of the reins. Accustomed to going all-out, they were thrown off stride, swinging too far out, heads tossing and teeth bared as they fought the restriction. Ferdo did his best to control them, but he had been trained to win and, like the team, he was unsettled.

Swinging back toward the Spine, he blocked the White chariot which, coming too close, was suddenly wreathed in flying splinters from its locked wheel. Red, seeing his chance, sent his team lunging toward the gap formed on the inside, a space barely wide enough to pass through, his offside horse slamming against the inner horse of the White team. For a moment it looked as if all three chariots would end in a pile of wreckage and then, suddenly, Red was clear.

The roar of the crowd rose from all sides.

"Belens! Belens! Belens for the Reds!"

Nero might be the first across the finishing line, but the spectators had no doubt as to who was the real winner.

As the gold chariot slowed, I rose and shouted, "Lucius! Lucius for the Greens! Lucius!"

A shout that reached the ears of Nero who turned and looked up at me.

"To the Greens!" I yelled again. "Lucius for the Greens!"

The colors were more than just identifying marks for the stables; they were representative of warring political factions, and my shouts had stirred the appropriate loyalties. Within seconds others had joined in, Belens's name was drowned out as every Green supporter strained his throat.

"Lucius! Lucius for the Greens! Lucius!"

Flushed, happy, Nero accepted the laurels of victory; then sent his team slowly around the track, one hand lifted as if he were a god dispensing favors. In a sense, he was. As he finally left the circuit and headed toward the stalls, a crowd of slaves ran over the sand. From baskets they hurled ivory tokens into the stands; each token entitled the holder to a gift of some kind.

"So he did it," mused Aquilia. "The Emperor of Rome lowered himself to the level of a common charioteer. Competing with slaves for an empty victory."

"Aquilia!"

"I know. Be careful. His spies and informers are everywhere and a loose word can lead to torture. But, Atilus, why did he do it?"

A question I couldn't answer. Nero was governed by whims and look a delight in outraging established opinion, but this seemed to be going too far. The Fathers of the City would never forgive the insult to their class. The Senate would be outraged. The great families would feel degraded. If Nero wanted to turn them against him, he could have chosen no better way.

But he was not a simpering fool who knew no better and neither was he insane, as Caligula had been. Willful, yes, with a child's unthinking cruelty, but his upbringing was responsible for that. Even so—why had he done it?

A question I dismissed as the trumpets sounded for the next race.

An hour later we left the Circus. Chariot racing had its devotees, but I was not among them, and Aquilia, conscious of her skin, had no desire to ruin its whiteness by too long an exposure to the sun.

Escorting her home and leaving with a promise of returning later, I made straight for the house I had bought on the slopes of Esquiline. It was large, luxurious, a home fit for a senator with vast estates or a merchant with many profitable interests, and I had filled it with rich furnishings and items of value. Attached to the house was a walled garden filled with a variety of trees and shrubs. Fountains filled the air with a soft tinkling, a sound now acting as an accompaniment to the harsher ringing of steel.

"In, boy, in! You have to be faster than that!"

Agonestes was dressed as if for the arena; the boy, if he was that, was wearing the equipment of a secutor.

"We'll try again," said the Greek, tiredly. "Now, as I

lift the net, try and anticipate where it will fall. Use the shield to block it, but remember that I've got the trident and will drive it into you if you give me the chance. Ready? Now!"

As training it was useless, but I could appreciate Agonestes's difficulty. It was like teaching a person to read; you first had to explain the characters. Now, slowly, he shifted the net, lifting it, casting it with a flick of his wrist, opening the mesh that fell in a filmy cloud over the other's helmet.

As the boy lifted his shield too high and too late, the trident darted in to rest blunted points against his chest.

"You're dead!" I called. "That blow would have killed you."

"Atilus!" Agonestes turned. "I didn't expect you back so soon."

"And I didn't expect to see you. How are things in Capua?"

"Later." He glanced at the boy. "You've come in good time. Felicio, this is Atilus Cindras. Atilus, meet Felicio Dillius." He added casually, "His father is high in the treasury."

A position which explained why the Greek was taking trouble with his son.

"This is an honor." The boy removed his helmet as he greeted me. "To have actually met the famous Atilus! I have heard my father speak of you."

"Nothing bad, I hope?"

"No. He considers you to be the finest gladiator of

our time. Certainly the one with most style. He's often talked about those women you trained for the arena."

"That was a long time ago."

"I know. Four years."

In the arena that could be a lifetime. And the incident with the women was one I did not wish to remember.

Lifting my hand I said, "See that post? The one covered with straw? Go over there and hit it. Use the full weight of your back and shoulders and make the chaff fly. Send that sword against it as if you were cutting down an enemy of Rome."

"This?" He looked dubiously at the heavy, blunted weapon in his hand.

"That. If you want to build up your sword arm, that's the way to do it. Keep at it until you're told to stop. Now, Felicio, move!"

Jerking my head at Agonestes, I led the way into the house. Inside it was cool and a slave brought us wine. "How long are you stuck with the boy?" I asked Agonestes.

"Until this evening, when a slave will come to escort him back home. Then, again, tomorrow, and after that, maybe until he gets bored."

"Why bother? So his father's rich, but what is that to you?"

Agonestes said dryly, "As you said, Atilus, his father is rich. He's crazed on the arena and would have undergone training as a gladiator if it hadn't been for a twisted spine. He might even have fought as a volunteer, and could even have won a few bouts and got it out of his system. It's happened."

But not often. Many volunteered to fight, and among them were the sons of patricians who were either bored or disinherited; but the devotees of the games either remained away from the sand or, if lured to participate, quickly died or found the lure irresistible.

"And the boy?"

"Felicio?" Agonestes shrugged. "I think his father's trying to live through him. Certainty he interested him in the arena when he was young enough to be taken to see the games and now, I think, he wants to see him fight and win in some small engagement. Not yet, of course, but when he's ready. As he's willing to pay for the trouble, I'm taking I can't object."

"His own son? The man must be mad!"

"He's a Roman and sometimes I think all Romans are mad. Do you think the boy is any good?"

"No." His body was too slight, his bones too frail, and despite his interest he lacked an inner fire, a determination to win, without which no fighter could survive. It could be instilled, given time, but how to take the son of a rich patrician and treat him as a slave? "Not as a swordsman," I amended. "With the net, perhaps, but his father wouldn't go for that and, in any case, I wouldn't bet on him."

"And me?"

I met his eyes and saw the question, the one each man carried within himself and could never escape. The clock measured a fighter's life. Agonestes was almost forty, an old age for many, too old for the normal gladiator. Yet he was my friend.

"On you, yes."

"If you bet on me you'd be a fool," he said flatly. "I haven't been in the arena for years and you know it. Not since we took out those women—and I wasn't fighting then. Time gets us all, Atilus. I'm no exception."

"You'd fight and you'd win." I finished my wine. "What do a few years matter? You've kept in condition and you are still as good as the best. A little older, perhaps, but what of that? You could take on any of a dozen I've seen lately, and have them downed before they knew what hit them."

It wasn't wholly a lie and I could see that he was pleased.

"Anyway," I added, "what does it matter? You're not going to fight again."

"What else?" His eyes darkened. "Live on your charity?"

"You have money."

"I had money," he corrected. "It's gone. Some bad investments and, well, other things."

Young men and, maybe, a few boys. I thought of the boy outside, but he was a true Roman, and would not yield himself to another man. For him, even if he'd had the inclination, it would have been easy to choose. For others it was not so easy. Looking at Agonestes, I felt a quick sympathy. Once so eagerly chased by wealthy patricians, it wasn't pleasant for him to have to do the chasing.

"You don't have to worry," I said. "This house is your home—use it as such." And before he could object I added, "When my ship comes home we'll all be rich."

"Your ship—any word as yet?"

It was the biggest investment and almost the biggest gamble I had ever undertaken. Nothing could beat the gamble of life itself, but this came close. I'd taken a half-share in a trading venture, paying hard-won gold for both vessel and cargo bound for the East. It would trade the goods of Rome for rare and exotic spices, silk, dyes, valuable animals, and anything else the captain decided would bring a profit. The cost had been high, but the potential profit was enormous.

"There were storms in the Aegean," said Agonestes quietly. "Sabinianus had word of them from a courier traveling from Ravenna to Miscenum. The seas were too rough for him to take passage. Your vessel may have had to run before the wind and taken shelter somewhere."

"Perhaps."

"Or—" He broke off, shaking his head. "Never mind. Your argosy will arrive in its own good time. But I can't depend on you forever."

"We'll be partners. Rome is full of opportunities and I'll stake you to a venture. We can speculate in land, buy some tenements and add a few extra floors, and there is always the animal trade in beasts for the arena. Look at Ofonius Tigellinus! Once he was a Sicilian horse-trader and now he is Prefect of the Praetorians."

"I know," said Agonestes. "Poor old Burrus was

barely cold when the Emperor filled his shoes with that crawling sycophant."

"But he got the position," I reminded. "Never mind how he climbed, he reached the top. And if a stinking dealer in horses could rise to command the Praetorians, then just think of how high a trained gladiator could rise if he put his mind to it. Don't look so glum, man. You'll never starve."

"No." He set down his wine. "I know you well enough for that, Atilus, but there is more to life than bread."

"And you'll have more," I promised. "Much more. We both will. Now let me hear no more about you getting old. Listening to you turns my hair gray."

"If it does, Atilus, there is always dye."

"And short-sighted women?"

"You'll never want for those, short-sighted or otherwise. You have the gift, Atilus. The face of a god and a body to match. Rome is covered with inscriptions from young girls who long for your embrace." Lifting the goblet, he spilled a few drops of wine on the floor. "That for the gods and the rest"—he drank—"to you. Now I'd better see how Felicio is getting on."

Satisfied, I moved through the house as Agonestes headed toward the garden, his face more relaxed now, his mood brighter because of my reassurance. Inside, Heraculis straightened from his examination of the sword I had brought from Aquilia's house and the bag of gold lying beside it.

"Take the one," I said, "and I'll cut off your hands

with the other."

"And hang them around my neck with a cord? Master, we aren't in the degenerate East but in Rome."

"That won't stop me."

"Did I say that it would? But, master, it is against the law to subject your slaves to cruel and unnatural punishments."

"You aren't a slave now and haven't been for years. Are there any messages?"

"Three." He lifted the fingers of one hand. "The Lady Amilia would like you to attend her on a journey she intends to make shortly to Narbonese Gaul. The fee for your protective services has not yet been settled."

"It won't be. Gaul is too far and the lady too ugly."

He lowered one finger. "Grassus Paciaecus extends an invitation for you to stay with him for a few days at—"

"No. I'm not keen on supplying what he wants. What else?"

"An invitation from the Great School for you to attend the banquet to be held in honor of Gallus Caecina on the occasion of his retirement."

"Gallus retiring?"

"So the message stated. It is by his own wish, I understand. It isn't for a while as yet, but I said that you would be there."

"You did right. Gallus retiring!" I shook my head; it seemed incredible. Another proof of the insidious passage of time. He had seemed as solid as the stones of the school itself—as well entrenched as the power of Rome. "I must send him a gift. Look for something both suitable and useful. And be generous."

"Of course, master. How about the sword the woman gave you? But, no, that would hardly do—she will probably expect you to use it soon."

I said flatly, "One day, Heraculis, I'm going to grab hold of your insolent tongue and tear it from your mouth. Now order the servants to prepare my bath."

The bath was of marble, set into the floor, warmed by air heated in a furnace. An expensive luxury, but one which I enjoyed. Now, wallowing in the steaming water, I felt myself relax. Even the momentary irritation caused by Heraculis's play on words turned to a wry amusement. The man took chances and, one day, he would probably take one too many, but he had little to fear from me and he knew it. As long as I didn't catch him cheating too heavily on the household accounts, I would tolerate his insolence—and none could better the ex-slave at the suggestive look and implied insult. Even when I had granted him his freedom after Verdalia had died, he had asked, with mock affront, how he was to live.

Leaning back, eyes closed, I could see his wrinkled face.

"You grant me freedom, master," he had said. "Freedom to do what? To starve? How am I to live at my age? Who will employ me? What shall I do?"

I solved the problem by simply paying him a wage and allowing him to continue as before, but now with greater authority.

But other problems remained. Agonestes had worried me with his talk of storms. The ship on which my fortune depended was long overdue. Storms could account for it; a wise captain would have sought shelter, and Massa Longinus was skilled at his trade, but there were other dangers. Illyrian pirates hunted the seas like famished wolves, uncharted reefs could rip out a bottom, brigands could swoop down from the hills and plunder a crippled vessel that had put into shore for repairs. And always there was the threat of sudden, unpredictable squalls, mutinies, and sickness.

Risks that could not be avoided, but that justified the high profits to be gained from the business.

Tomorrow, I decided, I would make sacrifice to the appropriate gods: Fortunata, Neptune, Jupiter Stator himself. It would do no harm and the priests would be glad of the offerings.

A touch on my shoulder jerked me awake. I looked up into a round, moon-like face.

Heraculis had bought a new slave from Etruria, more for his own comfort, I suspected, than for mine. She was a well-built girl with massive breasts and hips and buttocks to match. Her best feature was the mane of thick, lustrous hair, which rippled like an ebon waterfall to her waist.

"What is it, Fabia?"

She touched me again as if I were fragile glass. "Master, Heraculis told me to attend you."

He had dressed her for the part. She wore a short, loose robe, which fell just below her hips and gaped at the top to reveal the smooth curves of her naked flesh.

"What did that old goat tell you to do?"

"Simply to attend you, master." She added, quickly, "I am skilled at massage."

I doubted it. Her hands, broad, the fingers spatulate, looked more fitted to milk a cow, yet it would do no harm to let her try. I dried and lay on a couch and watched as she filled her palm with warm, scented oil. Deftly she began to rub it on me and then, as her confidence increased, her fingers gently massaged my muscles. Her skill surprised me.

"Where did you learn to do this, Fabia?"

"My old master at the farm used to suffer from cramps and he taught me how to ease them." Her hands lingered in the region of my hips. "But his body wasn't as nice as yours."

"No?"

"No, master. Yours is hard and firm and nice, even if it is scarred."

My scars didn't seem to bother her. I felt her hands on my back and shoulders. Heraculis had done well even if unintentionally. The girl had assets and I would see that she developed them. Trained, groomed, and taught a few graces, she would fetch a good price from the owner of a bath that catered to a select clientele— one that would appreciate both her skill at massage and her femininity.

"Master." She was breathing heavily, her fingers pressing hard. "If you would turn over and let me finish your stomach?"

It wouldn't stop at that and we both knew it. As if by accident, her breasts touched my shoulder and I could feel their soft invitation. Turning, I looked up at her; her mane of hair fell about my face, enveloping me in a gossamer cloud. The breasts bulging from her robe were like oiled bladders suspended above my mouth.

"Master!" Heraculis called from beyond the door, his voice urgent. Suddenly he burst into the room. "Master, a tribune of the Praetorians has arrived and demands your immediate attention!"

CHAPTER THREE

The tribune stood in the atrium, his face hidden as he studied a Grecian vase. He looked tall and splendid in a uniform of gold and crimson. He had come alone, which was a good sign—at least I was not to be put under immediate arrest—but why had he come at all? Had Aquilia's indiscreet remark been overheard and reported? Was I to be questioned? Then, straightening, he turned.

"Macer!"

"Did I startle you?" His face broke into a smile. "I'm sorry, Atilus, but your majordomo is such a ridiculous figure of a man that I had to play a joke. He must have a guilty conscience. It took so little to frighten him. I'd suggest you find an auditor to check the accounts. By the way, did I disturb anything?"

The experience I was about to enjoy could wait until another time. I didn't explain; to have done so would have been to tickle his rough, soldier's humor and provide a juicy scrap of gossip for the mess. Instead I studied him as he stood tall and proud before me.

"It's been a long time," he said, guessing my thoughts. "Six years since I saw you last?"

"Closer to five."

"And how long since we first met?" He answered his own question. "Almost twenty years, Atilus. A long time. But it looks as if you've done well for yourself."

I had a fine house, slaves, rich furnishings, all the appurtenances of a successful man, and all gained since I had seen him last. Obviously he had been away from Rome or he would not have been surprised. His smile widened when I asked where he'd been.

"Britain, Atilus, your old home. And the gods favored me. I was at the right place at the right time. You remember the uprising of the Iceni last year? Well, I saw action and plenty of it. I learned fast and climbed high. The next step will be to become a legate with my own legion. If the gods continue granting me their favor, it will be soon. Vespanian has promised his support and he is a man of his word. With him to back me and with Nero's consent, it will be accomplished."

"Your old ambition, Macer."

"Yes. Remember how we used to talk when we were boys? I was young, but even then I knew the real power of Rome lay in the legions and not in the Senate. Time has proved me right. Soon—" He broke off as if conscious he was saying too much.

"Atilus?"

"Nothing." I shook my head, dismissing old images: that of my mother lying dead, warriors speared and vomiting blood, children used as target for javelins. Things which belonged to the past and easily forgotten here in Rome. Verdalia had reminded me of them once, but she too was long dead and only a fool shed tears for ghosts. "I'm glad to hear of your good fortune, Macer, and pleased to see you again. Everything well with your family, I trust?"

"Father is dead," he said somberly. "Flavia, that greedy bitch, has remarried and is living in Spain. Gratus managed to get himself gored by a wild bull when handling a shipment of beasts. And Lucillia needs help. Which is why I had to return to Rome, but, frankly, Atilus, I was glad of the opportunity. Only in the heart of the Empire can a man gain the ear of those who can really help his cause."

Nero, of course, and others; influential senators, rich traders, wealthy families—all wanting favors and all willing to pay for them in one way or another. And, as an officer of the Praetorians, Macer was in a strong position.

"Nero gave me the appointment," he explained when I asked how he got it. "I'd done him a small service—and now I'm doing him another. Atilus, you are summoned to the palace."

"When?"

"At dusk." Macer looked through a window at the sky. "Which doesn't give us long to talk over old times."

At the palace we were received by an usher and guided into the inner courtyard, which had been set with benches and chairs arranged in a semicircle, facing pillars before which hung thick curtains. A mixed assembly sat in the improvised theater, and I recognized Dollitia Flavia, who lifted an arm and gestured for me to sit at her side. She had not improved with age, but cosmetics hid the signs of dissipation and, in the dusk, she still had beauty.

"So you too have been invited to the performance," she whispered. "I hope you're in strong stomach."

"Why? Is the Emperor—"

"In one of his moods? Only the gods can answer that, but certainly he is acting strange. You saw him at the Circus?" Then, as I nodded, she continued, "Now you're going to see him on the stage. Tomorrow you could see him trying to emulate Simon the Magician, perhaps. Who knows?"

"He couldn't be so stupid." Simon of Chaldea, boasting that he could fly like a bird, had jumped from a tall tower, only to be dashed to pieces on the ground. "Nero may be odd at times, but he isn't mad."

"Maybe not." She glanced at Macer, who was talking to a gray-haired senator. "Did your friend tell you how he gained his appointment to the Praetorians? No? I thought not. Well, you remember Octavia?"

I remembered the pale-faced young woman I had seen run from me as if she had seen a ghost.

"Yes, but should we talk about her?" We spoke in whispers, but listening ears could be sharp. "The Emperor was right to divorce her. Her adultery was proven beyond all doubt and she was barren."

Lies fed to the populace. Octavia had borne no child because she had died a virgin. Tormented slaves had provided the only evidence against her. Exiled to Pandataria, her days had been numbered.

But, for her, I felt no pity. She had been a fool. Twenty years had taught her nothing. Nero had wanted his freedom from the political marriage his late mother had arranged. Poppaea was swollen with his child and he was determined to marry her. Octavia had refused to cooperate, clinging to the outmoded loyalties of ancient Rome. Death was the price she had paid for her stupidity.

Had Macer dispatched her to the land of the dead?

An ambitious man would not hesitate to kill a young, defenseless girl, especially not when his own promotion depended on it. I looked toward Macer again; now he was talking to Seneca, who sat hunched in a chair with a robe spread over his knees. Beyond him Petronius whispered to a slave, and shortly afterward, some lamps illuminated the deep shadows of the courtyard.

Whatever performance Nero intended, he was certainly taking his time.

As, restless, I looked for a slave to order wine, music rose above the murmur of conversation and brought an immediate silence. It came from behind the pillars, a fair enough piece of melody, broken before it became tiresome by the abrupt parting of the curtains. Beyond them, through a veil of gauze, was a bedchamber illuminated with massed lamps set as if they were stars. On it, dressed and painted as a woman, Nero lounged languidly, waiting.

"It's a piece of his own," whispered Dollitia. "A sketch based on the legend of Cupid and Psyche. He asked my advice on how he should be dressed. Naturally he is taking the part of Psyche."

"And Cupid?"

"Pythagorus."

Nero's favorite, an ex-gladiator who, it was rumored, shared the Emperor's bed more often than Poppaea herself. Perhaps she didn't object; huge with child, she had gone to Antium to avoid the stifling summer heat of the city. She would have been more afraid of a woman catering to Nero's sexual whims than a man.

Now, as the music faded, Nero began to speak in a high, falsetto voice, wailing the fate that had led him to this place. The lights dimmed and from the shadows came the sounds of passion. As the lights brightened we could see Nero, alone but disheveled, rapturous over the lover who had come in the night. Three times and then the finale when Psyche yearned to see the face of her lover and broke her vow. As the lights brightened we saw Pythagorus, naked but for strips of leather, proud and busy acting the man. Nero, bent over beneath him, squealing in feigned protest, took the part of a woman.

The scene was greeted with extravagant applause by those watching, and I joined in loudly.

Nero, bathed and dressed in his gold and purple, joined the assembly to entertain us with a panegyric on the beauties of the sea as seen from the prow of a vessel heading into the harbor at Alexandria. Yielding to popular demand, he followed it with a song of his own composition and then, as an encore, played the lyre first accompanied by a flute player, then alone.

Ofonius Tigellinus came to join me. As he lifted his goblet of wine he said, "You did well today, Atilus. I like a man who knows what to do and when it should be done."

He was referring to my shouts in the Circus, of course. There would have been a group with leaders primed, but as in the arena, unless some had specific instructions, they would hang back waiting for a lead. I had given it to them.

"You are kind to say so, Prefect. Personally I admire a man with ambition."

"An attribute you share, I suspect." His eyes met mine over the rim of his lifted goblet; they were hard, direct, searching. "But a wise man recognizes his limitations."

A warning? If so, there was no need. The center of power held no attractions for me. Fame and position were gained at too high a price when both rested on the whim of a man who more and more displayed his contempt for the rules of established behavior.

"My ambition is small," I said. "Money, a house, some slaves, and a measure of comfort is all I need. That and the trust of the Emperor, together with the kindness of friends."

A smile creased his face and, nodding, he turned away.

A babble of voices rose to one side as a cluster of men and women discussed the races. Nero was in their center and I joined the group as a woman mentioned the fifth race.

"It was superb! Such grace! Such expert handling of the horses! Can genius have no end?"

"To a true artist all things are possible." A man, his face blotched with red patches, lifted his hands as if appealing to the gods. "Music, the dance, the stage, the whole world is his domain. And is not a track a stage? The pound of hoofs music? The sway of a chariot a dance? I had no doubt the Greens would win."

A shadow of anger spread over Nero's eyes.

Quickly I said, "You were fortunate to have such conviction. I did not. I backed the Reds for a hundred gold pieces."

"And lost?"

"Of course."

"But—" The man broke off, obviously considering me a fool. "Couldn't you tell? Didn't you know?"

"I am a gladiator," I said flatly. "I know the arena and I know something about the races. Not for one moment did I think that an untrained man could win. Today I saw the incredible happen, and the loss of the gold was worth it."

"Really?" Nero was pleased. "Did you think I rode well?"

"You were magnificent. The start was superb, a marvel of calculated judgment, and when you gained the lead you managed to hold it the whole distance. Frankly, I didn't think you would. Twice Ferdo almost overtook you and he was going all-out, but each time you managed to block his team. And, toward the last, it was neck and neck, with the best charioteer winning."

Shrugging, I added, "It was cheap at the price to watch a master at work."

"It wasn't easy," said Nero modestly. "But I did my best."

"More than your best." The woman, eager to pile on the flattery, bowed and knelt at his feet. "When you first appeared I thought that Apollo himself had descended to earth to show himself to us poor mortals. I wanted to kneel in worship and I do so now. Hail, Nero, gifted of the gods!"

"Hail!" The voices rose as others added their salutations. "Hail, great Caesar, god of Rome!"

Watching Nero's face, I restrained myself from joining them. Their reaction was natural; previous Emperors had been deified by the Senate, and Caligula hadn't even waited for death. He had publicly pronounced himself a god and had executed those who had failed to immediately recognize his divinity. Maybe Nero would follow his example.

Nero had noticed my silence. "And you, Atilus, can you not recognize a god?"

Quietly I said, "Can any man recognize a god who wishes to remain unobserved? If so, I am not one of them. But I can recognize a man gifted above all others. When you play, I listen to Orpheus himself. When you dance, the Graces are with you. Today you diminished the skills of men who have devoted their entire lives to the track. For a man to do such a thing is living proof of his genius. For a god to do them lessens their accomplishment. And, whiles kneeling at the feet of an artistic genius, I can only bow in humble awe before the altar of a god."

"Neatly said." Nero's smile was genuine. "And yet, who knows? At times I feel that I am touched with divinity." He smiled again as flattery rose about him like a cloud of verbal incense. "You think, Atilus, that I am capable of mastering anything to which I put my hand?"

"Indeed, yes, great Caesar."

"Today I raced in the Circus," he mused. "Tonight— well, only the gods can decide what is to be. Now let us enjoy the feast."

Reclining on a couch, I dipped my hands into a bowl of scented water proffered by a slave, allowing him to dry them on a napkin before making my choice of a vast assortment of dishes. Dormice had been seared and coated with honey. The tongues of larks, spiced and covered with a thin pastry, rested on a bed of fish eggs. Lampreys, sliced and smoked, rested in bowls of succulent jelly. Suckling pigs, stuffed with tiny sausages and puddings; chickens containing a paste of nuts and herbs; wild boars with gilded tusks; a plethora of meats, fish, birds, all accompanied by compotes formed into exotic shapes and pastries beyond counting both in number and variety.

The entertainment matched the food. A band of musicians accompanied a troupe of young girls dressed in filmy fabrics as they performed an intricate dance. A tall, well-built Circassian acted the part of Leda, manipulating a trained swan whose flapping wings accentuated rather than concealed her nakedness. A couple, the man wearing the hide and head of a bull, performed the ancient rite of love. Two naked wrestlers, their bodies covered with oil, gripped and panted as if they had been living statues. Two maidens from Judaea played an ancient game with monstrous phalli strapped to their loins, a third their mutual target. Nubians writhed to the sensuous beat of drums.

The titivation had its effect as the wine flowed and Bacchus ruled. An aging knight tripped as he rose, grabbing at a woman who had dropped her gown to expose her breasts. A couple, oblivious to those who watched, writhed with closed eyes and sobbing voices as, his body buried in hers, the man nuzzled her breasts. Others, yielding to the demands of Venus, threw aside all restraint as they turned the palace banqueting hall into the scene of an orgy.

"Atilus!" Dollitia Flavia reached toward me. "My darling! Atilus!"

Another saved me, gripping Dollitia around the waist from behind, pulling her away and turning her on her back as his hands delved beneath her stola. She responded, her arms lifting to wreath his neck as, forgotten, I moved away.

Petronius stood at the side of the chamber, his smile cynical as he watched the frenzied activity.

"An arena, Atilus," he said as I joined him. "One different from that you know and in which you are expert, but one just as deadly in its way. Here we see reputations being destroyed, affiliations threatened, old loyalties ended and new associations begun. Well, such is life and who are we to complain? To participate is better than to ignore. Pleasure is the sum total of human aspiration, for to gratify the senses is the only real achievement we can know. To touch, to feel, to see and taste and hear—aside from that, what is there? The answer, my friend, is nothing. So live while you may and take what enjoyment you can find."

The creed of a man who had done much and found little. Had he been forced to work in the mines or sweat under burdens in the fields, his affectations could have taken a different turn. Only the rich can sneer at joy— the poor know too little of it.

Nero was nowhere to be seen and, restless, I wandered from the hall. The rooms and passages were deserted, aside from a few slaves and the stolid Praetorians who stood guard. From a shadowed nook, I heard the sound of heavy breathing, and the sigh of a satisfied woman.

I entered a large room set with tables littered with scrolls and sheets of parchment. To one side, lying on a bench, was a shield, sword, and heap of armor. I found greaves, a cuirass, and kirtle of leather straps thickly studded with metal—armor designed from an ancient pattern.

"You like it, Atilus?" Nero stood behind me, a guard at his side. Waving the man to stand beyond the portal, he came to stand beside me. "It is similar in design to that worn by Achilles during the siege of Troy. Perhaps we could stage that combat in the arena one day. It would provide a good spectacle, don't you think?"

"The idea has merit, Caesar."

"If I decide to make my name in the arena, I shall wear armor of my own devising. See?" He delved into a chest, rising with a piece of equipment in his hand. "What d'you think of it?"

It was a protection for an arm and, if nothing else, it was beautifully made. Plates of metal, overlapping in diminishing circlets, riveted to underlying leather provided a good articulation. The ridges would hold and trap a sword, the thickness would protect the arm beneath.

"Total protection," said Nero. "Imagine a man dressed in armor like this all over. He would be able to walk and bend and move his arms, but nowhere would he be vulnerable to a sword or trident. He would be like Talos, a man of metal, invincible."

And he would destroy the games. The crowds wanted blood. They wanted to see flesh yield beneath the edge. Armored as Nero intended, a gladiator would fall from exhaustion, not wounds.

"A wonderful concept," I said enthusiastically. "It could even be extended to the military. Soldiers would enter battle far more confidently if they knew they couldn't be hurt."

"The weight would be against them, Atilus. It would be impossible to march for long wearing such armor. But in the arena—well, I shall see." Throwing the armor back into the chest, he abruptly changed the subject. Gesturing to the litter on the table he said, "What do you think of those?"

The sheets held plans of buildings and of a city I barely recognized as Rome. The walls were familiar, as was the great temple to Jupiter on Capitoline and the Circus set between the Aventine and Palatine hills, but the pattern of the rest was strange. The streets, which now twisted like snakes, were wide and straight running like arrows. One drawing in particular held my interest.

"Beautiful, isn't it." Nero stood beside me. His face was flushed and his breath smelt of wine, but his words were clear and the hand he rested on my shoulder was firm. "A palace based on the architectural genius of the ancient Greeks. A building that will fill all who behold it with an appreciation of the power and majesty of Rome. I shall call it my Golden Palace."

"It is magnificent," I said, and I meant it. "A home worthy of the greatest ruler the world has ever known."

"A man, Atilus?"

"A man among men, great Caesar. One who will set his mark on this age and time. One who will be remembered as long as one stone remains on an another."

"But a man?"

"As yet a man," I said cautiously. "Or a god who wishes to be known as one. But in the future, who can tell?"

"Divinity comes quickly at times," he said. "Look."

The coin he handed to me was fresh from the mint. A silver denarius which bore the likeness of Nero's head framed by a rayed crown. The attribute of the god of the sun. Even the most ignorant plebeian would get the message of divinity.

"I'm having them made for later circulation, Atilus. Now I want you to be honest. These"—his hand brushed the scattered plans and drawings—"what do you think of them?"

"They are ambitious," I said carefully. "The Golden Palace will be the wonder of the world. Yet it will take a lot of space to build it. And even more space will be required for the other alterations."

"A detail." He was impatient for my praise. "But the plans?"

"If they could be turned into a city, then all men would envy those chosen to live in it. But the cost—"

"Will be high," he admitted. "But the money can be raised with persuasion. I am pleased you could accept my invitation, Atilus. I remember how you guarded me before I gained the purple, how you saved my life. A man, even an Emperor, needs friends. As a god needs priests to do his bidding."

"Command, Caesar, and I will obey!"

"Of course, Atilus, you are a faithful subject." His hand squeezed my shoulder. "Now, let us return to the festivities."

CHAPTER FOUR

It was past dawn when I left the palace and my eyes were gritty from fatigue. Walking down the slopes of Palatine, I tried to determine the expanse that would have to be cleared to accommodate Nero's proposed new buildings. It was obvious the area would be vast, and hundreds of present structures would have to be razed before construction could begin.

Soon he would recognize the difficulties and the opposition his plans would arouse. The drawings would be put away, and Nero would find something else to titillate his jaded senses. Hopefully, he would also put away the armor and his intention to fight as a gladiator.

The prospect had chilled me, and even while I praised it, I hoped the gods would deter him before it was too late. A charioteer could lose a race without loss aside from his prize money, but a gladiator could only lose at the expense of his life. And, should he decide to win, what horrible tortures would be meted out to him for having killed the Emperor?

These were further proofs of Nero's lurking madness, or perhaps more subtle manifestations of his warped genius? For a genius he was, even if only in the realm of devious planning. His talk had hinted of the aid I could give him and the trust he placed in me. A gladiator knew how to kill and a few dead men would persuade others to find money for his buildings and support his plans against any opposition from the Senate.

Had Macer, who had already proven himself a capable assassin, been sent to invite me to the palace to make an assassin of me also? Had he suggested that I might be perfect for the role?

I didn't worry long over these thoughts. Soon I would be far away from the danger of Nero's plotting intrigues. When my ship came in, I would be a rich man, rich enough to quit the sand forever, to return to Britain, buy an estate, and become a lord of the Iceni.

When I reached my house and entered the atrium, I found an officer waiting there for me. He wore a naval insignia.

Saluting he said, "Atilus Cindras?"

"Yes."

"Owner of the *Regulus*?"

"Yes. Who are you?"

"Drusus Venutius, captain of the *Endymon*. I've just returned from patrolling the Aegean and I'm now on my way to report to the Emperor. I have a man with me who has something of importance to tell you. He's waiting in the garden." His hand dropped with unexpected warmth on my shoulder. "I'm sorry."

"My ship?"

"Yes."

"Gone?" Then as he nodded, I said, "But how? How?"

Tubero had the answer. He was old, burned and wrinkled by the sun; his clothes were in rags and his feet bare. An ugly wound marred the side of his head where skin had been slashed away to the bone. I ordered wine and, as he sipped it, he told me what had happened.

"We had a good trip at first. Massa knew his business and took full advantage of the winds. We headed south and made good time, calling at Alexandria, then moving up the coast to Joppa, Ptolemais, Tyre, and Selucia. It was a good trip and we traded well. We had one of the best cargoes I've known."

"And?"

"We took the usual route home. In the Aegean we ran into storms and had to scud before the wind. We lost the mast and had to put in for repairs, but Massa was careful and chose a deserted coast. The repairs took longer than we thought and I guess we must have been spotted by some wandering goat herders."

Agonestes, who had joined us, said sharply, "Didn't you keep watch? Surely Massa Longinus would have set a guard? The man was supposed to be an experienced captain."

"We had lost men in the storm." Tubero drank more wine. "But Massa did his best. We scoured the area and found nothing, but those herders have eyes like hawks and can crawl like snakes when they want to remain unseen. They must have sent word to pirates, because they were waiting for us when we finally set sail. Two galleys came at us like wolves. We tried to run and almost made it, but the wind fell and we stood no chance against oars. Even so, we made a stand." He lifted an arm to his wound.

"But it was no use. They came from both sides. I saw Massa go down with his head split open with an ax and ducked just in time to save my own. I dropped and pretended to be dead—it was all I could do. They stripped me and dumped me overboard with the others and I managed to tie myself to some floating wreckage. For three days and two nights I drifted, and then I was picked up by a patrol galley. We've been at Misenum br two days, then moved up to Ostia." He added quietly, "I walked from there."

Fourteen miles in the hot sun with a head that must have ached every inch of the way. Hanging to the tail of the officer's horse, perhaps, if the man had been kind. Coming to bring me news I didn't want to hear and yet had to know.

"Agonestes, take care of him. Give him food and clothes and money, then send him on his way."

The sea had opened and swallowed my fortune. Earlier, in my ignorance, I had been confident that I would never again have to tread the sand. My certainty must have offended the gods, for now the fortune I had hoped to increase was lost.

And more had gone with it.

Bad news travels fast, and the following morning a

representative of the Probi banking house came to visit me.

"My dear Atilus, you must forgive this intrusion, but the matter is somewhat important."

"To whom?"

"To us both. It is not of my doing, you understand, but I have partners and they are concerned. They send their regrets as to your loss."

"Give them my thanks. And?"

"It is the matter of the loan made against the house. They think it best that it be cleared." I shouted for Heraculis. He came at once; probably he had been listening behind the door.

"The loan from Probi. When is it due to be paid?"

"In five months." He added quickly, "They cannot foreclose as long as the monthly interest is paid."

"Such a short time," murmured the Greek. "Surely it would be more convenient to settle the matter now? The interest would, of course, be waived."

"The interest will be paid," I said curtly. "The principal also when it is due."

He left after some more argument. I knew that others would follow, sharks snapping at a crippled swimmer, each eager to avoid loss. In the small room I used as a study I frowned over the accounts.

"Can I meet the Probi loan?"

"Not without selling the house," said Heraculis. "And there are other debts." His finger tapped the parchment. "You see?"

Trained to keep accounts, I was no stranger to

figures, but I didn't like what I saw. Money had come in, but money had gone out even faster and large bills were owing which would have to be paid.

Heraculis shrugged when I grumbled.

"Master, you were too generous to those women who survived when you fought Helvidius. To each you gave money for a home, farm, and husband."

"A dowry. They earned it."

Again the shrug. "And there was that large gift you gave to Agonestes."

"At the time I gave you your freedom," I pointed out. "Do you begrudge that too? If I hadn't been so generous, I could have sold you for a hundred sesterces."

He said with quiet dignity, "I am old and far from strong, yet I have certain skills which I am sure make me worth more than a single gold piece."

As I well knew, even a slave had pride and I had been cruel. Squeezing his arm I said, "You're worth a hundred times as much, Heraculis, and I know it. It would serve me right if you were to walk off and leave me to it. Now, what are we going to do?"

"We could economize. Your gift to Gallus Caecina, for example. I could cancel it."

"No."

"You told me to be generous, master. It will cost over a hundred gold pieces."

"He's worth it. Make economies elsewhere. On the food, for example. You and the rest must be living like kings."

"And your guests?" He was ironic. "Shall they arrive

to be feasted on bread and water?"

Unwittingly I had drifted into a trap, spending money without regard, relying on the riches my investment would bring. That hope was gone. Now, unless I was to sell up and vanish into obscurity, I would have to take another gamble.

I told Agonestes what I intended to do. He listened to me with a growing look of concern.

"Fight? Atilus, you intend to go into the arena?"

"Why not?" I met his eyes and didn't like what I saw. "You think I'm past it?"

"No, but—"

"I've a reputation and can cash in on it. I'll get a high fee and the prizes should be good."

"If you win—yes."

"I'll win." I looked at him, then at Heraculis. "But I don't went either of you to tell anyone that. Instead, you're going to tell them that I'm off form. I've been drinking too heavily and sleeping with too many women. I'm soft and no real match for any experienced man. Don't overdo it and don't make it obvious. Just lay the groundwork and, when I'm matched, start betting against me—you know what needs to be done."

"But you really mean to fight?" Heraculis asked.

"Of course, what else can I do?"

The gods who had so cruelly dashed my hopes now were kind and shortened my waiting. In Antium Poppaea gave birth to a daughter and to celebrate the event Nero ordered a great spectacle, which he would personally attend. For days before the event Rome was littered with placards announcing the games and the names of those who would be contending, my own prominent among them. I exercised from dawn to dusk with the help of Agonestes, falling into bed at night after being massaged by Fabia, too exhausted to take advantage of the delights she offered.

A few days before the display I eased a little, aware of the danger of passing my peak. I let myself be seen in the wine shops and, on more than one occasion, appeared to be hopelessly drunk. On the eve of the display I attended the customary feast.

"Darling!" A painted harridan threw her arms over my shoulder, her free hand stretching down lower. "A gold piece if you will stab me with your sword."

"No."

"Let me kiss you then. Let me feel you in my mouth."

"Try another." Impatiently I pushed her away. A man halted beside me.

"Atilus, you are my favorite. Come with me and let us enjoy the love made famous by Greece."

He was old, withered, his bones sharp beneath the skin, his face like a yellowed skull. But he wore a toga with a red stripe, and men with such authority had to be handled with discretion.

Gently I said, "Not tonight, Domine. An affliction of the bowels, you understand?"

He blinked at the lie, then, to my relief, passed on to accost another. A man facing me across the table grinned as he lowered his goblet.

"Neatly done, Atilus, I must remember that." Brinno

was an essedarius and would fight from a chariot. As we wouldn't be facing each other, he could afford to relax. Casually he reached for a scrap of spiced bread and tore into it with strong white teeth. "I heard about your loss. Too bad."

"It happens."

"All the time," he agreed. "A man tries to get ahead and the gods play him dirty."

"Greed," I said. "Not the gods."

"Maybe. How have you been making out?"

"Well enough." I glanced down the table, saw people watching, and pretended to drink an entire bowl of wine.

"Do you know anything about Sacrata?"

"The retiarius? You facing him?" He frowned at my nod. "A bad one, that. A man goes in to win, but he doesn't have to be vicious about it. Get your man down and let the crowd give the verdict, is what I say. Kill him if you have to, but if not, give him a chance. Well, Sacrata doesn't work that way. I saw him blind a man once, a Thracian, and there was no need. He was going down, sica thrown to one side, shield wide, but the bastard couldn't leave it at that. He had to put in the trident and take out the eyes." Taking another sip of wine Brinno added, "A pity. The crowd voted him life."

"Nice," I said. "I'll remember that. Maybe I'll get the chance to treat him the same. Any weaknesses?"

"Watch his foot. I don't like betraying a man, but the quicker that bastard gets it, the better. So watch his right foot. Just before he makes his cast he twists out his heel. He'll make a dozen feints, maybe, but when you see that heel go out you'll know it's for real."

Gallus Caecina called to me as I left the feast. He was not alone.

"You've heard about my retirement, Atilus?"

"I have, but why retire? You could last another decade."

"That's what Junius and I have been telling him," said Flavius. He was a short, squat man who belonged to the Draclan School as Junius belonged to the Gallic. "Maybe you can convince him, Atilus. We can't."

"A man should know when he's had enough," said Gallus. "I could last a while longer yet, but what then? I want to leave while there's still life left in me. A small farm somewhere, a few slaves, and I'll take things easy."

I said, "You'll be lost. After the first few weeks you won't know what to do with yourself. You'll miss the life."

"What life? Teaching a bunch of raw slaves how to use a sword? Lashing them on, shouting, keeping them in line? Getting them on the sand and watching as they forget all they've been taught and go down at the first exchange? Up all hours, having to keep fit, having to stay sober? No. From now on I'm going to enjoy myself. Good food, soft women, strong wine. A simple, easy life."

"Live like a cabbage and you'll die like one," said Flavius. "Come on, Junius, let's leave the poor old man and get some real fun. If you want us, Gallus, we'll be at the Concordia."

He looked at me as they left, then said quietly, "You should think about what I said, Atilus. No man can go on forever."

"Are you saying that I'm getting old?"

"You aren't getting younger. It's been a long time since you won the rudis and, as the years pass, things happen. Small things and you wouldn't notice them, but they are there. A slowness, the need for more time in which to think, old scars robbing you of needed mobility. If men didn't get old, Atilus, we'd have gladiators fighting in their nineties. We'd be like the gods, immortal. Do you think you're a god?"

"No, of course not."

"Then take a hint. You've been spreading your fights and that's good. But spread them too far and you'll lose more than you think. Better still get out while you can." His hand dropped to my shoulder. "I like you, Atilus, I always have. You're a good fighter and you kill quick and clean. I'd hate to see your guts spilled on the sand."

"You won't."

"I've heard that before from men as good as you," he said bleakly. "They wanted that one more fight, that one extra prize. They wanted the adulation, to remain on the top with women chasing them and love-sick girls scrawling their names on every wall. They forgot that, always, there is someone waiting to pull you down." His hand fell from my shoulder. "Don't make the same mistake they did. Don't believe you can't lose."

CHAPTER FIVE

I was scheduled to fight late in the afternoon; Sacrata and I were to be a high point in the day's events. But I arrived early to commence my preparations. I'd seen the ritual build-up of blood thirst often enough, and rather than watch beasts and tyros being slain to enliven the frenzy of the spectators, I preferred to relax.

Heraculis had accompanied me and had reserved a quiet corner in one of the rooms. I lay on a bench and managed to doze for a while, then woke to wash and sip some wine. I'd eaten nothing since early morning, when I'd had a breakfast of raw eggs; milk, and porridge, but still I didn't have much of an appetite.

"How long?"

"Soon, now." Heraculis was grave. "You're due after the next event."

I'd dozed longer than I'd thought. Now I went through a series of exercises to loosen my muscles, conscious of tension and irritated at my mental condition. Always, before a fight, there was this strain and nervous stress; the imagination which helped me to win also anticipated what would happen should I lose, but now it seemed worse than at any other time. Perhaps Gallus had been right, I had spread my fights too wide apart. Perhaps I was growing soft, becoming a prey to fear.

"The odds?"

Heraculis swallowed before answering. "Two to one against you."

A bad sign if a man believed in omens. The advantage was always with the retiarius as the betting showed. Five to three in his favor was normal; against one with my reputation the odds should have been evens or less. That they weren't could be proof that the man was better than I suspected.

"We could be responsible for that," said Heraculis, trying to sound cheerful. "According to us you're as good as beaten."

He was too politic, I noted, to use the word *dead*, but that's what I'd be if I went down. The money I'd given Aquilia Sabina to back me would be lost. Yet it was true that our manipulations must have altered the odds. Well, so much for omens; now I had to get into the right frame of mind for combat.

Deliberately I thought of the past, of my mother and what had been done to her, of my life as a slave. Of Verdalia and how she had died.

A Roman had killed her, ruining that superb body and robbing me of its pleasures. Romans had murdered my mother. Romans had enslaved me. Sacrata was a product of Rome. As a Roman he would die.

As the trumpets blared their summons I ran through the Gate of Life.

Sacrata was waiting. He was a tall, lithe man, with

eyes like those of a tiger. The net in his hand moved slowly from side to side, bright sparkles flashing from the gilded lead pellets weighting the edge of the mesh. More sunlight blazed from the polished tines of the trident, winking like stars from the sharpened barbs with their needle-like points. On his left shoulder the galerus shone as if made of silver—metal to protect the vulnerable flesh.

"Get him, Atilus!" shouted a woman. "Stab him with your sword today, and stab me tonight with your other sword!"

"Atilus!" another shouted. "Put him down and ride me till dawn!"

There was time for me to lift my sword in greeting. As the cheers died a man answered the invitation with a yell to my opponent.

"Spill his guts, Sacrata! Let's see the color of his tripe!"

Others joined in, voices raised in a blur of noise whim faded and then became a hush as we settled into position We stood alone; neither of us needed trainers with their hot irons and straps.

"So we meet at last, Atilus," said Sacrata. "I've wondered for a long time who is the better of us."

Now he would find out. I watched through the lattice of my helmet as he stepped toward me, still at a safe distance, his voice soft as he purred the traditional chant.

"I do not hunt you, Gaul. I seek a fish. Why do you swim away?"

Before the words were out of his mouth I attacked.

With a rush, I thrust at his swarthy face. Like an eel he darted to one side, metal ringing as he thrust with the trident, the barbs glancing from my lowered helmet. As they hit I lashed upward at the wooden shaft, knocking it aside, advancing within reach of the weapon as, again, I thrust at the naked body before me.

Backing, he swept the net at my feet in an effort to trap an ankle and pull me down. I jumped over it and landed safe—and saw the outward twist of his right heel.

Like a spreading cloud, the net fell toward my helmet, but forewarned, I avoided it just in time. Leaping aside, I blocked it with a lift of my shield, expecting the trident to come thrusting at my exposed body, meeting it when it came with the sword, sending the edge between the tines, twisting and pushing the weapon aside as I retreated.

The first exchange revealed his strength and speed. He was good. Younger than I, unhampered by shield, helmet, or armor, he wouldn't be easy to take.

"Atilus!" shouted my supporters. "Atilus!"

"Get him, Sacrata!" yelled others. "Rip him open!"

The sun had heated my helmet so that sweat ran over my face and stung my eyes despite the strip of cotton I'd wound around my head. The stench of the arena rose like the effluvium of a sewer as we trod in the mess left by previous combats—slippery patches which formed a constant danger, but which could not be wholly avoided.

As we fought my mind worked like a machine. I remembered old lessons, previous experiences, the knowledge won with the blood of men.

The greater mobility which gave a retiarius his greatest advantage could only be made full use of while he kept his distance. The trident had a longer range than the sword. The net could be thrown and, once engulfed in it, a man's chances were small. The straight-edged gladius lacked the cutting power of the curved blade of a sica and, in order to thrust, a secutor had to get in close.

A fact Sacrata was fully aware of, and he kept his distance, forcing me to follow, trying to wear me down.

Deliberately I slowed. While still advancing I took longer to cover the distance between us. The lift of my sword was not as fast, the swing of my shield as I blocked the net grew wider each time. And I breathed harshly, deeply, panting as I dodged.

Things that he must have noticed and that, I hoped, he would misread.

"Getting weary, Atilus?" His voice was a sneer. "You should have retired while you had the chance. Well, never mind, soon you'll have all the rest you can use. An eternity of it."

Confidently he slowed in turn, matching my pace, playing to the crowd, and laughing as he dodged my clumsy attacks. The laugh turned into a curse as, seeing my chance, I trod on the net he swept at my ankles. I trapped it against his pull, holding him prisoner by the thong which held it attached to his wrist.

Two steps and I was close, my greave and shield turned toward him, my sword swinging up to parry the thrust of the trident in his left hand. Metal rang and then I was through, striking before he could rip the net free and run past me. The tip of my blade caught the left side of his torso and cut a long furrow over his naked chest.

"Habet!" As one the crowd rose, shouting as blood shone red in the sunlight. "He's wounded!"

The wound was little more than a scratch, but there had been no time to poise myself for a thrust or to put my weight behind the cut. Even so, the air shook to the sound of my name.

"Atilus! Atilus! Atilus!"

Snarling like an animal, Sacrata backed away. Then, without warning, he lunged toward me, passing on my shield side and escaping the reach of my sword. As he passed I swung wide the shield, slamming it against his arm. Jumping free of the net, I went in again, giving him no chance to recover, Blood spurted as I slashed at his arm, more as I thrust at his waist.

Then he was away, running over the sand, his body streaked with crimson.

"Atilus!" A woman rose, shrieking. "Kill him! Kill!"

A tyro would have done his best to obey immediately. I also would obey, but in my own good time. Sacrata was hurt, but he was not yet crippled. And hurt, he was more dangerous than before.

He spat as I edged toward him. "More tricks, Atilus? Is that the way you fight? You belong in a dark alley, not an arena."

Insults I ignored and wasted no breath in returning. Instead I watched his hands, his eyes, his feet. The right foot, which was now dug into the sand. The heel, which twisted outward.

Lifting the shield to block the anticipated cast of the net, I exposed myself to the thrust of his trident. Too late I recognized my mistake. His pattern was deliberately created to be broken in time of need. Sacrata had been cunning and I had been a fool. No retiarius of his standing would have risen so high had he signaled his every move.

Instinct saved me—that and the trained, unthinking reaction gained over the years. As sunlight flashed from the points I twisted, letting them rake across my stomach instead of burying themselves in my guts. I felt the rip, the burn, the warm wetness of blood as it flowed over my belt to puddle on the sand. As Sacrata lurched forward, carried by the momentum of his thrust, I sent the edge of my sword hard against his thigh. Dropping, he rolled, one hand digging into the sand, a yellow cloud flying toward my face as he threw the handful of grit. Stinging grains passed through the lattice of my helmet and caught me in both eyes as, too late, I turned.

Blinded, I felt the net drop over me, the mesh hard against the rim of my helmet, pulling as, confident of victory now, Sacrata ran to keep it taut between himself and me.

I should have died then. I would have died had he

jerked, then come in with the trident, but he wanted to make the most of his success and he wasted time pulling me around. Time that gave me a chance.

To have tried to cut the net would have left me open. To have followed the pull and run at Sacrata would have been to commit suicide. I had to escape, to gain the opportunity to clear my eyes. The fool had given me the chance, but the only way to take advantage of it was to discard my helmet.

A yell rose from the stands as my helmet fell to the ground, the sound turning into ugly jeers as I ran from my opponent. Eyes cleared, I turned back to face him.

"His eyes, Sacrata! Get his eyes!"

My face was now exposed to both the pellets weighting the net and the barbs of his weapon. I ducked as the net lashed like a whip toward me, the lead pellets stinging my shoulders and rattling on my shield. The trident followed, aimed high, lifting higher as I beat it upward with my sword. Lunging in, I cut, the point catching his cheek, laying the flesh open to the bone, the steel dragging down to the mouth.

"Atilus!" the crowd shrieked in pleasure. "In! Finish him! Kill!"

The end had to come soon. Sacrata was hurt and losing blood. I was, too, but only in a minor degree. However, I was tiring, and the loss of the helmet put me at a serious disadvantage. To guard my head and eyes I would have to lift my shield, a defense which would leave my left thigh exposed and, worse, block my vision.

Sacrata lifted his hand toward his ruined face.

"You'll pay for this, you barbarian scum! I'll have your eyes and leave you blind. I'll spear your cheeks and tear your ears. I'll cripple you so that no woman will ever want to look at you again. I hope they give you life, Atilus. Death would be a mercy!"

He stepped forward to meet me, the net lashing through the air, again aimed at my face as I'd anticipated. This time, instead of lifting my shield, I ducked, rising beneath the trident, my shoulder hitting the shaft. The net rose before me, a coil looping around my neck, and as Sacrata drew back the trident, I stepped forward with sword poised to strike.

One step—and I felt my foot slip on a patch of blood. As I was thrown off balance, I felt the sword knocked from my hand, saw the trident lifted. I turned as I hit the sand so that the vicious points missed my loins. Instead they ripped into my side.

"He's down!" The crowd shouted the obvious. "Sacrata! Sacrata!"

The hero of the moment, the idol of those who watched. But he wasn't finished yet. Having fallen down, I should have been left to the mercy of the crowd. Instead he ripped free the trident and aimed it at my eyes.

"Blind," he said. "I promised to blind you. Well, Atilus, here it comes!"

I had no sword, blood was spouting from my side, and sharp steel was poised over my eyes, but I still had the shield and I used it. It swung up and across, a blunt-edged ax that smashed against his kneecap, shattering bone. As it landed I rolled, feeling the tines rip into my scalp and grate against the bone of my skull. As Sacrata fell on top of me, I snatched the dagger from his belt and drove it deep into his groin.

For a moment we lay face to face as if both of us were dead; then, rising, I lifted the dagger and my stained hand toward Nero.

"Atilus!" The crowd, driven hysterical by the abrupt turn of fortune, showered the sand with fans, veils, coins, wine jars, anything they could find. "Atilus! Atilus!"

With the shouts came derision for the fallen; hands were outstretched, thumbs jerking downward. Only a few fluttered handkerchiefs and held up their thumbs as a sign they wanted life to be granted. Nero ignored these as, his own hand extended, he gave the signal to kill.

CHAPTER SIX

The walk back to the Gate of Life lasted an eternity. My progress was marked by a thick trail of blood, yet I forced myself to keep going, to square my shoulders and even to smile and wave at the crowd. The pride of a gladiator made him contemptuous of wounds. Romans loved such a display of courage.

Heraculis waited in the opening, two strong slaves at his side.

"The infirmary, quickly," he snapped. "And be gentle."

The first instruction was unnecessary, the second ignored. Like a side of beef I was lifted and dumped on a stone couch and stripped. Water was sloshed over my wounds as a physician waited to examine them by the light of a guttering lamp held by an assistant.

"These will heal." He touched my scalp and the slashes on my stomach. "And so will these." The bruises caused by the lash of pellets together with a minor cut on the shoulder I hadn't noticed. "These are another matter."

I heaved as his fingers probed. Inside it felt as if I'd been filled with fire, the flames searing like glowing charcoal, the burn of red-hot irons.

"It hurts, eh?" The physician grunted. "A bad place, Atilus. A little to the right and the hammer would be a mercy." He gave me a goblet of wine heavily laced with opium.

Heraculis said impatiently, "Can't you stop the bleeding? It's running out of him like wine from a slit skin."

"All in good time." The physician, a Greek, refused to be hurried and wanted no advice from anyone not in the profession. "The loss of blood will cool his inner fevers," he explained. "When air meets earth there is always a danger of fire. Atilus is earth; air has entered his body; it must be expelled or absorbed before the wounds are sealed." He added casually, "Also, the flow of blood will help to wash out any dirt which may be in them." He made another examination, grunting, then signaled to a slave. "Bring the irons!"

They came glowing from the brazier as a slave thrust a wad of leather between my teeth. I felt the heat, smelt the odor of hot metal, then reared as it touched my flesh. Red-hot iron at each of the wounds, searing, burning, sealing the openings. It hurt more than the thrust of the trident itself, the ripping agony as the tines had been jerked free. The pain seemed to last forever, mounting, filling the world with a spreading redness, a glow edged with black.

"Master?" Heraculis was staring down at me, his eyes anxious. "Master?"

"I'm all right." I felt weak and my head was pounding.

The leather wad had been removed and a slave stood by with a bucket of water. At my nod he threw it over me. It was cold. As his assistants wound strips of linen around my waist, I said to the physician, "How long?"

"Before you fight again?" He shrugged. "That depends on how fast you heal. At a guess I'd say at least a few months."

"As long as that?"

"The barbs ripped your insides," he explained. "There is internal damage which will take time to mend. If you tear open the inner wounds before they are properly healed you will suffer for it. Live quietly, sacrifice to the gods and, if they so decide, you will live to fight again."

I would have to fight again within weeks, not months. The summer would be over then and I still had debts to settle.

A litter carried me home. Fabia fussed as she put me to bed. The opium had dulled me so that I slept. When I awoke, Agonestes was at my side. He gave me a little water and when I asked for wine he shook his head.

"No, Atilus, Hazeal won't permit it."

"Hazeal?"

"The physician I've hired to take care of you. He's from Smyrna and has a good reputation. Now just rest and don't worry. Aquilia has given me the money you won and sends her regards and her hopes for your quick recovery. It was she who recommended the physician. Now just rest and leave things to me."

"I'll be all right."

"Of course." His eyes held less conviction than his voice. "It will only take time. Now drink this."

It was a thin broth with a familiar, pungent taste. "More opium?"

"You need rest, Atilus. If you turn and twist about you'll do more damage. Now drink it down." He watched as I obeyed, then said gently, "How do you feel?"

"Tired." Strength had drained out of me with the blood I had lost and I seemed to be in a daze, floating as if on a cloud. "But I'll be all right soon, Agonestes. A few weeks and I'll be fighting again."

"Perhaps."

"I must."

"I know, but we'll have to wait and see. Hazeal is afraid there could be complications."

The doctor paid a visit a few days later. He was a small Jew with shrewd eyes and a thin mouth, which he pursed as he examined me. The rips on my stomach and scalp were sore and festering, the cut on my shoulder little better. He bathed them, clipping away the hair on my head and shaving my stomach, then coating the wounds with a noxious salve. He grunted as he looked at the cuts in my side. The flesh around them was an angry red, the skin taut; the scabs that had formed over the burns oozed a yellow pus. I winced as he probed.

"It hurts?" He frowned at my nod. "Badly?"

"I could live without it."

"I must know," he said patiently. "I am aware that it

is the custom for gladiators to make light of their pain, but I must have a guide. This now." He pressed. "Did that hurt more than this?"

"No!" I reared on the bed as his fingers sent fire lancing through me.

"As I suspected," he said. "There is an accumulation of fluid building up within the area. A mass of poison that must be dispersed. It may be necessary for me to open the wounds in order to relieve the pressure. We'll wait a few days to be sure."

Days in which I grew more and more detached from the things around me, lying in a semi-sleep interspersed with dreams, vagaries, flashes of light, and darkness. Barely was I aware of Fabia as she bathed me, changing the sheets on which I lay, the material sodden with sweat from my fevered body. Pain lived in my side and sent legions to attack the flesh of my scalp, stomach, and shoulder. I burned, throwing back the covers, begging for water, which was given in sips together with foul-tasting nostrums. Voices like the whispers of ghosts echoed around me as faces, yellow in the lamplight, came close to vanish, to hover as if wreathed in incense.

"I learned something about Sacrata. It was his habit to keep his trident buried in the putrefying body of a dog." Agonestes was bitter. "He wanted to make sure that no one would survive him."

"I suspected as much." Hazeal, thoughtful, loomed close. "The wounds must be opened and drained. Have you slaves to hold him?"

I moved through strange regions and relived old events. A man, his face distorted, died as my sword found his heart. Another, his face slashed, screamed as he fell. More appeared, a stream of men I had fought and killed in the sun, fell to writhe and die on the sand. A roar seemed to engulf the world.

"Atilus! Atilus! Atilus!"

The shrieks of the crowd. The voice of Rome. A voice demanding blood.

I screamed as pain tore at my side.

"Atilus?" The voice was worried. "Atilus?"

I strained against the hands that held me. Agonestes was looking down at me; his head was wreathed in a nimbus of light so that he resembled a god. Beads of sweat dripped from his nose and chin to splash on my cheeks.

"Atilus?"

"What—" I writhed as pain again tore at me. I tasted blood and screamed, all pride forgotten, as I descended into Hades. I was being butchered, red-hot knives sliced into my tender flesh, claws raked at every nerve. Pain rose to encompass the world.

"Hurry!" Agonestes was sharp. "Hurry!"

"It is done." Hazeal, his robe splashed with blood and streaks of yellow slime, his hands equally grimed, joined the Greek in my field of vision. "I've lanced the wounds and installed drains. Now we can only wait."

Again, I drifted into a place of dreams.

Years before, a man I met at a pre-combat feast had told me that, when asleep, a man's soul left his body to wander through time and space. How else could one explain the meetings with the dead? Only when the spirit was freed could such things happen and now, close to death as I was, those I met seemed very real.

Again I was a boy standing in the stronghold at Brentwood, seeing Caractacus ride through the gate, hearing the screams as the men of the legions appeared to kill and kill again to make Britain a province of Rome.

And again I saw a face beneath my own, one convulsed with passion as Flavia engulfed my body and drew the seed from my loins. A face that turned into that of Getia, which in turn became that of Verdalia.

"Atilus, my darling," she whispered. "Why do you keep me waiting? Join me and let us know again the pleasure we shared. Remember how warm my body was, how soft, how enticing. Come to me, my lover, embrace me, take me and again make me your own."

Verdalia's face was replaced by another, painted with woad, hair hanging loose as it framed a mask of hate. My mother.

"Live, Atilus! Live!"

She stood before me, hands lifted into fists, her eyes blazing with the hate she had felt when lying helpless she had been raped and then murdered.

"Live, Atilus! Live!"

Live to fight and avenge the fallen. A command sent by the gods and one I had to obey. Groaning, I turned and felt a hand resting lightly on my forehead. A broad hand, firm yet gentle, cool against the burning skin.

"Oh, master, live! Please, my love, live! Live, Atilus, my darling! Live!"

The touch of lips against my own, the pressure of soft fullness against my naked torso. Opening my eyes, I saw a broad, moon-like face, the cheeks wet with tears. A face framed by a curtain of hair, which swept over rounded shoulders and prominent breasts.

"Fabia?"

"Master!" She jumped back, staring at me, her eyes wide in the lamplight. "You've come back to us—may the gods be thanked!"

"Fabia, please, some water."

She gave it to me, supporting my head as I sipped the tepid fluid from an earthenware bowl. Through her robe I could feel the breast, which rested against my cheek, the nipple hard and firm. As she settled me back I slept again, waking to sunlight that brightened the wall, to the touch of Hazeal's hand.

"How do you feel?"

"Weak. Weak and hungry."

"Good. A sharp appetite is a sure sign of returning health." He touched my scalp, shoulder, and stomach. "Any pain?"

"No."

"And here?" He pressed at my side, pursing his lips as I flinched. "To be expected, but it will pass. I've removed the drains, and healing is progressing as it should. For weeks you have lain in fever. Now it has broken. God was kind to you, Atilus.

"Now you need to regain your strength. First some

broth with eggs beaten in milk and a little bread to accustom your stomach to food. Then some lean red meat, chicken, cheese, good wine, and some honey."

"No blood?"

"Yes, if you wish, and if you can stomach it, as much raw liver as you can swallow."

His voice was casual and I guessed that he didn't think much of the gladiator's belief that the blood of animals could replace the blood lost in combat. But it was the first time I'd heard anyone recommend raw liver.

Sitting upright, I clutched at the sides of the bed as the room spun and nausea swept over me.

"You must take things carefully," warned Hazeal as he supported me. "You've lost a great deal of blood and you are weak. Any sudden exertion could rip open the wounds. If you lose more blood you will die. You understand?"

"Yes."

"I hope so," he said and added with dry humor, "I'd like you to live at least long enough for me to collect my fee."

Fabia took charge after the physician left, storming at Heraculis, feeding me as she would a child and tending me like a mother. Hazeal had left some nostrums, which she insisted on administering despite my objections to their foul taste. She rewarded me with rich pastries and concoctions of eggs and honey and eggs beaten with pounded raw meats, which she insisted had the virtue of restoring vital energies.

She could have been right; certainly I seemed to gain strength and weight, and within two weeks I was sitting in the garden.

I was there when Gallus Caecina came to visit me. He sat beside me beneath a laurel, regretting that I'd not been able to attend his farewell banquet and touching discreetly on the matter of the gift I had sent him.

"I've heard rumors, Atilus," he said gruffly. "If things are hard with you, then—"

"No."

"I can't refuse a gift," he said. "Not if you refuse to take it back. But there's nothing to stop me from offering you a loan."

"You haven't the money to spare." Rising, I took a few steps, fighting dizziness as I hastily sat down. "That farm you mentioned will cost more than you think. You'll need beasts and materials, and slaves have to be fed."

"I haven't bought it yet."

"Why not?" I laughed as he made no answer. "Be honest now, you really don't want to leave Rome. Am I right?"

"The place gets into the blood," he admitted. "But my mind's made up. It's just a matter of deciding on the place. When you retire, Atilus, where will you go?"

"I'm not retiring."

"No? I thought—" He broke off, looking at his hands.

"How about somewhere in Campania?"

"Why not Pompeii?" I reached for a plate of meat and bread, obeying Fabia's orders that I eat at every opportunity. "The amphitheater's been closed for years now, so you'd be free of temptation. You could get a place overlooking the sea and live quietly and simply. Property will be cheap after the earthquake. And if you get restless for the arena you could always visit Capua."

"I won't get restless."

"You will." I swallowed the meat I was chewing and took a mouthful of wine. "You'll listen to the talk and long for the smell of oil and sweat and the sound of clashing steel."

He fell silent, staring into his goblet, then said abruptly, "Atilus, when I get my place will you come in with me?"

"As a sleeping partner, you mean?"

"No." His eyes were direct as they met my own. "A place to which you could retire."

Patiently I said, "I'm not retiring, Gallus. I've been hurt, but it isn't the first time and I'll get over it. Soon I'll be back in the arena fighting as well as before."

"Do you really believe that?"

"Of course. It's the truth."

"Maybe." He swallowed his wine and rose. "But remember what I told you, Atilus. A wise man knows when he's had enough."

CHAPTER SEVEN

In the weeks that followed, good food had restored flesh to my bones. Exercise would turn that meat into muscle, but the sharp edge I needed was slow to return. I grew tired too quickly, the dull ache in my side was a constant nagging, and the supple litheness of my body seemed to be gone forever.

Doggedly I persisted, training, working until I almost dropped, resting to work again. And always I was conscious of the passing time, the weeks that slipped into months, the shortening days, which presaged the coming of winter.

"Atilus, take it easy!" Agonestes lowered his net and slammed the blunted points of his trident into the dirt. "You've had enough for today."

"No. We'll keep at it."

"For what purpose? I could have killed you a dozen times in the past hour. You're tired and getting tireder. Get sense, man. First you must heal."

The wounds had closed, and aside from the puckered flesh I was whole again, but the damage, as Hazeal reminded me, was within. Summoned by Agonestes, he frowned as he examined me.

"The body is a chalice designed and created by God and filled with the blood that is the life," he explained. "Once break it and let that life escape, then only God and time can restore it. God has been good to you, but there has been insufficient time. Next year you should be whole again; now you are delaying a full recovery by your insistence on exercise."

"How am I to live until next year?"

"Ask that of a cripple begging for bread," he snapped curtly. "I am only a physician." More softly, he added, "I understand how you feel, but be thankful you are alive and whole. Don't try to walk before you are strong enough to crawl. Go among the poor. See the maimed, the deformed, and the diseased and give thanks to your gods that you are not as they."

I followed his advice and bought beasts to sacrifice to Jupiter and made other offerings to the gods favored by my profession. I took long walks also, strengthening my legs, again becoming a part of the city. Yet my troubles remained; a gladiator who could not fight was nothing. And time was against me.

Together with Heraculis I brooded over the accounts. Except for Fabia, the slaves had been sold together with other household items. The interest on the loan had been met, but the principal had yet to be paid. The money I had won had vanished in fees for the physician, expensive nostrums, rich foods, and the general upkeep of the house, together with the settlement of pressing bills.

Agonestes tried to help. "I can get a fight, Atilus. A

lanista I know can arrange it. There's a small munera in Fundi next week and I should win something."

"No."

"Why not? We need the money."

"I need you alive more. Agonestes, don't be a fool. You'd go down and you know it." I saw his flush, the sudden hardening of his face, and remembered his pride. "If you fight, then so will I."

"That's stupid. You aren't fit."

"Fit enough to beat you!" I glared at him. "Let's put it to the test!"

Each day we had practiced, yet I could never be sure that he was exerting himself to the full. He could have allowed me to seem better than I was in an effort to restore my confidence, but now, as we faced each other, there would be no deception.

Dressed, little stabs of pain coming from my side, the shield weighting my arm, the helmet a cramping weight on my head, I edged forward as I had done so many times before. The first cast I blocked, attacking in turn, missing when I should have hit, recovering with painful slowness. Again Agonestes cast the net, his trident accompanying the attack as he slammed the points at my side, the flesh exposed as, like a tyro, I lifted my shield too high. A simple attack to block and yet, again, I was too slow. Sweat ran down my face, my legs felt like water. A weakness that brought an impatient anger and a rage-induced strength.

With a burst I was against him, my shield pushing him back, my sword lifted to ring with a harsh, metallic chime as it slipped between the tines of his trident, the blade rasping as, seeking to trap it, he twisted the barbs. The move left him open to the renewed thrust of my shield. I released my grip on the sword to snatch at his dagger and to hold it against his throat.

"Very good! Atilus, you are remarkable!"

I turned at the sound of clapping. A young man stood watching us, a patrician, his hair curled, his toga spotless. Heraculis stepped forward to announce the visitor.

"Master, this is Livius Titus Valerius. Domine, this is Atilus Cindras and his friend Agonestes."

"The Greek retiarius?" The tilt of the young man's head was casual. "A dead man now had he been in the arena. A neat trick, Atilus. I don't remember having seen it before."

Removing my helmet, I said, "We were testing to see if it could be done."

"And?"

"I would never advise it. Even with Agonestes cooperating, there were difficulties. You observed his deliberate slowness, of course?"

"His slowness?"

"First his positioning of the trident to allow me to place my sword. Then the maintaining of his position in order to enable me to get close. The twist up and outward as I released the blade. In an ordinary combat he would have backed and thrown his arm across the dagger. Two steps and I would have been at his mercy."

I was lying, but Agonestes was a friend and not to

be demeaned.

Now he said, "I'll bathe, Atilus."

"And think?"

"For a few days, at least." An answer which meant nothing; he still intended to fight and, if he fought, he would die. Our bout had made me certain of that.

"You must forgive the intrusion, Atilus," said Livius as the Greek vanished into the house. "I've only just arrived back in Rome and, hearing you were hurt, I had to come and see how you were getting on. I am more pleased than I can tell you to see that you are up and about. And ready to fight, eh?" His smile held a sensuous pleasure. "I shall never forgive myself for having been absent when you met Sacrata. The opportunity to watch good sword-work is rare. The Emperor himself speaks highly of you. I think it only fair to tell you that you are one of his favorites."

A bag of gold would have been of more value than the empty compliment, but I smiled as if he had given me pearls.

"It was gracious of him to have mentioned me. How are Poppaea and the child?"

"Both are well. The girl has been named Claudia Augusta and already she promises to match the beauty of her mother. If, with that beauty, she manages to combine the artistic genius of her father—what a woman the world will know!"

"A goddess," I said seriously. "Rome will be her temple."

I felt his eyes search my face as, deliberately, I

studied a leaf on a shrub. As I looked for mildew he looked for mockery, but I had been close to Nero too long to allow my feelings to show. Bluntly I asked why he had come.

"To see you, my friend. I was concerned, as are others of your acquaintance, Aquilia Sabina for one."

"And?"

He chose to misunderstand. "Well, now, let me see. There is Cadius Publius, who is suffering from a rather distressing internal complaint at the present and is thinking of retiring to his estates in Lucania. And Dollitia Flavia, who has found it best to leave Rome. And—"

"I don't want a list of people I know," I interrupted. "Why, aside from a touching interest in my health, have you visited me?"

"To bring you an invitation, of course." His hand lifted in a gesture I had seen before: a mannerism affected by Nero. "From Aquilia Sabina. She will expect you at dusk."

As I entered the atrium, Aquilia came forward to greet me, looking as I remembered, tall and impressive in a stola of shimmering silk, her hands extended to grasp my own.

"Atilus! My darling! How wonderful to see you again!"

"And you, Aquilia?"

"You have been away so long."

I said dryly, "But I did not travel far."

"To the Underworld and back," she said. "Far enough

for any man to travel. Much farther than my own journey to Syracuse. Did you wonder why I had not visited you? My darling, I was away in distant Sicily, but I offered regularly to the gods for your recovery. Now sit and tell me all that has happened since we last met. Were you pleased with the physician I recommended?" She gave me no time to answer. "Darling! I've been so worried about you!"

Worried enough, perhaps, to have sent Livius to see if I had been maimed before extending the invitation. It would have been typical of her. Hating deformity, she would not have wanted to resume acquaintance with a man who was abhorrent to her sensibilities.

"Atilus?" Her hands were soft as they rested on my own.

"Have you missed me?"

"Of course."

"And?" She frowned at my lack of response. "Are you angry that I did not come to visit you? But, my darling, I was in Syracuse." She edged closer, her body warm with sensuous heat, a ringlet of hair touching my cheek. "Such a dreadful place and the sun was so hot. Put your arm around me, darling." Then, as I made no effort to obey, she said, "Atilus, what is wrong?"

"I have worries."

"I know." Her tone was light and casual. "Your health. Your lost investment. The debt on your house. But you have no need for worry, darling. Not as long as you have me."

A promise, but I wanted more than words. "Aquilia,

will you lend me—"

"Hush!" Her fingers stopped my words, resting on my lips, the gold of the rings she wore cold against my skin. "Later, darling, we can talk business. Now I want to see if you can still fight."

Her bedroom was adorned like a temple dedicated to the gods of Greece, the cold marble softened by touches of warmth: vases filled with colorful blooms, bright fabrics in reds and oranges, ambers and yellows. Incense fumed from a brazier and yellow lamp-light touched the covers of the wide bed, ruby glints reflected from tinted glass containing fat candles. Red and yellow: the colors of blood and sand. Fitting hues for the arena of her bed. Around it the crowd in the shape of statues with painted, enigmatic eyes watched.

She sighed as my arms closed around her. She turned to face me, her eyes closed, her hands questing, her sharp nails dug into my flesh as, like a warm, moist cloud, she engulfed me.

"Atilus! Atilus, my love!"

We strained, locked in a battle I had fought so many times before. The tinted light softened the lines of her face and gave her body a youthful sheen. Beneath the skin her muscles writhed, bunching, smoothing as she forced herself against me.

"Darling!"

Her eyes were open now, smeared with streaks of antimony, the whites yellowed, the irises as black as the jet of her hair. Her lips met mine and fastened with an aching hunger, tongue thrusting, thighs lifting to clamp around my waist, her heels pressing hard against my buttocks as she held me close against her, gasping as she felt my eruption match her own.

Afterward, we lay together sipping from goblets of wine. "Atilus, where could I ever find another like you?"

"You flatter me, Aquilia."

"No." She faced me, her eyes direct. "I'm no stupid girl to be enamored of a gladiator's fame. And I've known enough men to be able to form an opinion. You are special. Too special to waste your life on the sand."

"So?"

"So something must be arranged. I told you, my darling you have no need to worry." She stretched like a contented cat. "When the others arrive we can settle it. Until then, my darling, we can enjoy the moment."

A time for love, for caresses, for me to bathe while maids attended to her hair. Waiting in the atrium, I greeted the first guest to arrive. It was Drusillius Augustus, whom I'd met at the Circus Maximus. He smiled with genuine pleasure.

"Atilus, I'm glad to see you around. That was a dirty trick Sacrata played on you."

"The sand?"

"That, yes, and I later heard about the rest. A vile thing to do. Not even barbarians poison their weapons. It is good that he is dead."

The other guest arrived as Aquilia joined us. Livius was as I'd last seen him.

"So we meet again, Atilus. It's good to see you,

Drusillius. Well, Aquilia, do we eat or do we first discuss business?"

Smiling, she said, "We can do both, Livius. Talk and eat at the same time. I've ordered only a simple repast, but it will serve, I think. And good conversation will provide an excellent sauce."

The meal was far from simple, but I avoided the more exotic foods and only toyed with the resinous Greek wine. As slaves brought water for us to wash our hands and cleared away the dishes, Aquilia gestured for the attendants to leave.

The talk, as yet, had been of trifles, and I had added little to it. Instead, I studied the others. Aquilia I knew and Drusillius held little mystery, but Livius was an enigma.

Now, with brusque impatience, he said, "To business. Drusillius, will you begin? If Atilus agrees we can settle the details immediately."

Taking an orange from a bowl, I peeled it and lifted a segment to my lips. "Agree to what?"

"Atilus, I've watched you fight," said Drusillius. "You have a talent which should not be wasted. Your reputation is good and you are at the peak of your fame." Pausing, he added quietly, "It is probably the best time possible for you to retire."

"What!"

"An undefeated champion retains his glamour. One who has had to beg for his life is never the same in the eyes of the public. You know that, Atilus, as well as I. Now is the best time for you to leave the arena."

I said tightly, "In moments now you are going to tell me that I'm too old. That I'm past it. That I'll go out on the sand again only to face defeat."

"No," said Drusillius. "I would never tell you that, but it is in your mind or you would never have mentioned it. Sacrata almost killed you. Another might succeed. Give it enough time and another must succeed. I'm suggesting an alternative. It would be to your profit and ours to form a partnership."

"Such as?"

"That you work with us and for us at all times," said Livius quickly.

The segment of orange slipped down my throat. Taking another I said, "As what?"

"A lanista."

From him it was a dirty word. To any patrician such a man was beyond contempt, worse even than the prostitutes who plied their trade in the open, who used any convenient corner to satisfy their clients.

Aquilia said, "There is money to be made, Atilus, and you need money."

"And you've done the work before," added Livius. "You were instrumental in introducing women to fight as gladiators."

"That was by the Emperor's command."

"Even so, you have the experience. And you were foolish not to have continued with your school. Female gladiators are no longer a rarity, and others have gained the fortune that could have been yours. Do you want to throw away another opportunity?"

The orange had turned sour. Impatiently I threw it aside. "A lanista. Is that the best you can offer me?"

"Money, security, release from the necessity of having to fight in the arena." Livius tapped his finger against his couch as he enumerated the advantages. "Freedom, Atilus, from the trap that is closing around you. The Probi are not noted for their generosity; they will strip you unless the loan is repaid. You can be saved from that if you agree to work for us."

"With us," corrected Drusillius quickly. "Work with us as a partner."

Alone they couldn't do it. They lacked both the experience and the knowledge, both of which I could provide. And social pressure would ruin them if they even tried to work in the open.

It was a demonstration of the hypocrisy of Rome. Aquilia's wealth came from the tenements she owned. Drusillius dealt in military contracts. Livius, younger, would be the one providing the drive and acting, perhaps, for others eager for high profits. And he knew what was wanted.

"Good, ruthless fighters, Atilus. Men trained and clever at their trade. You could pick them, hold them back, use them to the greatest profit. The aim is quality, not merely quantity."

Men to fight in private displays and enter the public arenas when conditions were right to arrange the bets. I didn't have to be told that it would be up to me to arrange things to be sure they would gain the largest advantage.

"Atilus?" Aquilia looked at me, and I could tell from her eyes that, if I turned down this offer, it would be the last she would make. "Are you interested?"

"In a partnership? Of course, but as yet I've not heard how large my share will be."

We argued for an hour and twice I thought I'd gone too far, but each time they saw my point of view. The house, all debts paid, would be mine for use as a school. All expenses would be paid and I would take a fifth of the clear profit. The arrangement suited me; Agonestes and Heraculis would be sure of employment, I would be kept, and there were always ways to make a modest extra on the expenses.

We sealed the bargain in wine and, later, I gave special thanks to Aquilia. As dawn lightened the bedroom she whispered, "Atilus, my darling, will you always love me?"

"Of course, dearest. Of course."

All lanistae were liars.

CHAPTER EIGHT

Petilius Slavius sipped at his wine and said slowly, "Well, I don't know, Atilus. Verax is good. He's one of the best and I don't want to lose him. I've spent a lot of time and money on that boy and it's time I collected. Don't forget he's had eleven fights and won each time."

"Ten wins and a draw," I corrected. "He was *stans missus*[1] the time before last."

"So he drew one." Petilius shrugged. "But he didn't go down and have to beg for his life, did he? That man's a first-class fighter and they don't come cheap."

Good men never did, and I couldn't blame him for doing his best to raise the price. Calling for more wine, I leaned back and looked at the shadowed interior of the tavern. Around us, seated at rough tables, men sprawled on benches drinking their wine from crude bowls and gnawing at lumps of bread dipped in honey or oil. It was a rough place, as befitted the town. Vesontio wasn't much more than a huddle of buildings set on the Rhone, a stopping point for the river traffic.

Petilius was typical of his kind. His clothing was

---

1. A tie.

rough, his tunic stained with dirt and wine, his leather sandals scuffed and cracked. He had a half-dozen gladiators in his familia, and their keep must have been a problem.

He said, "I'm not greedy, Atilus, and I'd like to see the boy get on. He is wasted in the provinces, he belongs in Rome, but a man has to look after himself. How about a hundred gold pieces?"

"He's yours to sell?"

"Of course." He grunted at my suspicion of his honesty. "A slave trained by Julius Scipo at the school in Trier. They teach them hard there and he knows his business. He's going cheap and you know it. In Rome he'd fetch three times what I'm asking."

Perhaps, but I'd heard that claim too often before. Every lanista swore that his familia contained some of the best gladiators, whom he would sell at a loss out of sheer love for me and respect for my reputation. Such flattery I discounted, knowing it for what it was. When it came to trading, a lanista had few equals and no superiors.

Now, to change the subject, I said, "How have things been with you?"

"Hard," he admitted. "I'd be a fool to tell you otherwise. Last winter was bad and I lost two men from the cold. If it hadn't been for some private work and a little arranged betting I don't know how I'd have lasted until the spring. I did well at Trier, though. The garrison likes plenty of action and those Germans—they have aren't much good with a gladius. They like the broadsword, and each time they take a swing they leave themselves wide open to a thrust. It was all rough stuff with very little skill. Still, it's a living."

One that had become my own. I traveled hard and far in search of usable material, haggling, buying, arranging bouts, and making frequent trips back to Rome, where Heraculis kept the books and managed the house. The work had restored my strength and vigor, as well as supplying a stream of gold. Now, with Agonestes, I was touring the area, buying, using, taking only the best back to Rome.

Petilius looked mournfully into his near-empty bowl.

"You're a hard man, Atilus. I can't blame you for that, but we independents are being squeezed all the time. How can a man compete with the Imperial schools? To take raw slaves and train them for two years takes more money than an ordinary man can raise. Even Julius Scipo finds it hard going, and he has the monopoly of the area and can get cheap captives to work with. I have to use what I can find. When a man like me gets hold of a fighter like Verax, it's a gift from the gods. I tell you honestly, Atilus, it hurts me just to think of letting him go. And I'll be frank, you couldn't offer me enough to part with him if I had any chance of taking him to Rome."

"I like to hear you talk like that, Petilius. A man should have a regard for his fighters, and you are a credit to the profession. Some more wine?" I refilled his bowl. "And I'm going to help you. Verax is good and you could earn with him. I want you to gain a little for the trouble you've taken with him. So drink up and we'll call it a day."

"You don't want to see him?"

"Petilius, I don't want to rob you." I paused long enough for him to regret a wasted opportunity, then said casually, "Of course, while I'm here, there's no harm in looking at him. But there's no hurry. Let's have some wine."

Two drinks later Petilius took me to the shed in which he housed his gladiators. One was lying on his back, his chest slashed. The damp straw on which he rested was moldering and stank of manure. On a bale of hay another nursed a wounded arm and thigh: he was a retiarius who would be lucky to win another fight and, from the look in his eyes, he knew it. The man I wanted was punching a sack full of grain, the meaty impact of his fists loud in the confines of the shed. Naked aside from a cloth around his waist, his body was bunched with muscle and bore only a few, minor scars.

A myrmillo and a promising one. He turned as I dropped my hand on his shoulder.

"Domine?"

"Take off that cloth and bend over. I want to see your backside."

The buttocks bore only a couple of scars from old burns, and the firmly rounded flesh was free of the welts raised by the lash of straps. A sign that he was a willing fighter and did not have to be beaten into battle.

That was a point in his favor. His face was another: the nose was sharply defined, the cheeks broad, the eyes deepset under heavy brows. A third asset was his skull. It was wide, thick-boned, the ears flat, as his thick neck was mounted on massive shoulders. He could easily withstand the weight of a helmet and the blows it would take.

"Open your mouth and show me your teeth." Bad teeth could cause pain and distraction. Broken ones meant he could have trouble with his food and so be prey to stomach pains and indigestion. "You didn't win your last fight but one. Why not?"

"The man I fought was too good for me. I couldn't beat him down."

Petilius said quickly, "He was up against an old hand, Atilus. A *primus palus*."

"A first-class fighter? In Trier?"

"He was after some easy pickings and was touring the provinces. The boy did well not to go down."

I said flatly, "Fifty pieces."

"Atilus! If you want to rob me, use a dagger at my throat! A hundred at least and not a sesterce less. Verax is like a son to me—don't ask me to give away my blood."

"Sixty—and I'm being generous."

We settled for eighty and were both satisfied. I could have beat him down a little more, but a good reputation was worth the difference. The local magistrate certified the change in ownership and, dressed in a ragged tunic, Verax accompanied me to the inn where

Agonestes was waiting. I ordered him a plate of food and left him to eat while I consulted with Agonestes.

"No luck, Atilus," he said. "That retiarius I went to look at would have been jeered from the sand and the Thracian was little better. Neither is worth your time."

"Did you arrange for transportation?"

"We can get passage on a barge leaving tomorrow. It will take us down the river to the coast."

"To Lyons," I corrected. "We may be able to pick up something at the amphitheater there. As yet this trip has cost us money and brought little hope of profit."

Aside from Verax, I'd bought a retiarius and a pair of Thracians, none of them outstanding, but each worth at least a fee and maybe a prize if they were lucky. They were housed in a stable, a warm, dry, comfortable place. Slaves they might be, but they were also fighters, and no man treated like a mindless beast could be expected to give his best in the arena. Taking Verax to join them, I gave my usual speech.

"You belong to me now and I don't want you to forget it. If you try to escape, you will be crucified. If you attack me or any other, you will be treated the same. No exceptions. When I give an order, you jump to obey it or I'll have the flesh scourged from your backs. That's the bad side. The good is this. Work hard and do your best and you'll be well-fed, well-treated, given a woman now and again, and maybe some other comforts, Keep winning in the arena and you'll keep living. Fall and you die. Those who keep winning will be taken to Rome, and once there you'll have women chasing you and the adulation of the crowd." Pausing, I added, "And you can win your freedom. Gain the rudis and you can't be made to fight again, but I'll add a bonus. Once the wooden sword is yours, I'll give you a certificate of manumission to go with it. Think about that. You'll be free to go where you like, when you like, do as you like. All you have to do is keep winning."

One of the Thracians said, "Master, when do we leave this place?"

"Tomorrow."

"And fight?"

"Soon." I looked at him. "Why? Are you in a hurry to die?"

"Not to die, master, to win. To enjoy those comforts you mentioned."

His answer showed the right spirit. Most lanistae tended to ignore their slaves and neglect their comfort, but I had a different system. To fight well, they had to be encouraged, and to treat them as human beings was a good way to do it. Also, a close association bred a sense of trust and a readiness to accept and follow advice. No man, nursing a sense of grievance, could concentrate fully on his opponent. Hate, correctly directed, was a useful tool, but the hate had to be for the man who was trying to kill him, not for the one who had sent him out to fight.

"I'll send in food," I said. "You can wash in the yard. If any of you have troubles, come and talk to me about them. Understood?"

As I left I heard one of them say, "A good man,

Scylax. We're fortunate."

"Can any lanista be good?"

"Atilus is. I've heard of him. He was a slave himself once and perhaps he remembers how it felt. And he means it when he promised our freedom if we gain the rudis."

That hope would keep them fighting like demons, and some of them could even gain the coveted wooden sword and the freedom I had promised would go with it.

At dusk I made my way to a small house at the edge of the town. The painted phallus showed what it was. The doorman, a maimed slave, grunted as he passed me through, then scuttled off to fetch the woman who ran the place. She leered as she saw me.

"Well, my handsome warrior, come to flesh your sword? I've a variety of delights for your entertainment. A girl from Syria or one from Gaul? I've a German who has yet to be touched and a dark-haired beauty from Spain. Or," she suggested, "perhaps you would like a young and agile boy?" She blinked as I told her what I wanted. "Something for slaves? How many?"

"Four."

"One should be enough. I've a girl who could take on a legion and they can ride her all night. A good worker and young too. You want to try her first?"

The girl was neither young nor good in any sense of the word, and I'd decided that one wouldn't be enough. A pair would give variety and stop any arguments. When drained, the fighters would spend a quiet night and would be no trouble from then on.

I settled on a blonde from Germany and a dark-haired witch from Spain. Neither was particularly attractive, but both were clean and had some touches of femininity in their figures. Beating down their owner's asking price and reminding her that I wanted only to hire them for the night, I gave each a denarius as a bonus and sent them together with a flagon of wine to the stables.

Then I took a walk along the river, watching the reflection of stars in the water, hearing the occasional splash of a fish. In the gloom, barges loomed like ancient beasts of legend, the mutter of slaves mingled with the rattle of dice, the occasional cry of triumph rising as did the curse of defeat. Some fishermen sitting on the bank returned my greeting, and a wine shop, hugging the edge of the wharf, attracted me with its lights.

As I stepped into the doorway I heard a crash, the yell of a man, a woman spitting out words in an almost forgotten tongue. It was the Iceni dialect of Britain.

"Roman pig! Touch me again and I'll have your eyes!"

A young woman stood against the far wall, a knife in her hand, the point aimed at the face of the man who stood before her. He was roughly dressed and obviously came from one of the barges. His hand cradled the side of his head, blood and wine running between his fingers. More wine stained his tunic and a broken flagon lay at his feet.

As he took a step forward, she spat, "By the sacred

oaks I mean it! Come closer and I'll be the last thing you ever see!"

Again she'd spoken in Iceni and the man didn't understand. But there was no mistaking the fury in her eyes, the savage intent of her distorted features, the knife that stabbed forward as she spoke.

"She's mad!" The man half-turned to the owner of the place, who stood behind his counter. Wine-filled amphorae were aligned on the rack behind him. "Mad, I tell you! She tried to kill me—you all saw it."

"Call the Watch," suggested one of the dozen others in the place. "They'll take care of her."

"There's no need for that." The owner, a burly man with a broken nose, carefully put aside the amphora he was holding. "I can handle her."

"How?" I spoke from where I stood just within the door. "Can you take that knife away from her without getting hurt?"

"Can you?"

Without answering I walked toward the girl. She watched me, probing the knife toward me.

In Iceni I said, "Don't be a fool. If you cut your master you could be crucified."

"Roman filth!"

"Not Roman. I'm a Briton like yourself. Now be sensible and give me that knife."

"You, a Briton?" She sneered, looking at my tunic, the gold bands gleaming on my wrists and arms. "Do you think to trick me? Stand back!" The knife moved in little circles. "I mean what I say!"

I could take her, but she was like a serpent poised to strike. She was no slut screaming empty defiance. Women of the Iceni knew how to fight, and a knife was their favorite weapon.

In Latin I said, "One of you behind me. Get a pitcher of wine and throw it at her. Quickly!"

She understood me and I saw her eyes follow a man who went to obey. Before they could return to my face I'd moved in. Too late she tried to stab at my eyes, snarling as my arm slammed against the inside of her wrist, my hand catching the fingers that held the blade, twisting as my other hand, closed into a fist, slammed at her jaw. It was a hard blow, but not hard enough to break the bone or even to knock her unconscious. Dazed, she sagged, the knife falling to the floor, only my grip on her wrist holding her upright.

"The bitch!" The owner, brave now that all danger was past, came hustling toward us. "I'll have the skin off her back for this. I'll flog her until she can't stand, and then I'll flog her some more. The stinking barbarian! The savage! She's been nothing but trouble since the day I bought her."

"A Briton," said one of the others. "They make poor slaves."

Another added, "You wasted your money there, Lupus. Not even the brothel would want a piece of skin and bone like her."

Suspended from my hand, she weighed little more than a child. The flesh I gripped was thin over the bone, and as she stared at me through the tangled mane of her hair, I could see the pinched features, the prominent cheekbones, the eyes ringed with purple smudges.

She wore a coarse gown of stained and soiled sacking, ripped in places and redolent of grease and rancid oil. With a jerk I tore it from her shoulders and looked at the welts crisscrossing her back.

"You've whipped her before."

"Often," the owner agreed. "But it does little good. She's recalcitrant. She's even threatened my life and I've a scar to prove she attacked me."

"He's lying," she said in Iceni. "He tried to rape me and I told him what I'd do if he did. A man would have taken me, but this Roman scum was afraid."

"What's she saying?" The owner reached out to grab her, grunting as I knocked aside his hand. "What lies is she telling now?"

"No lies." I pointed to her back. "I think I'd better report this to the magistrate."

"She's my property. I've a right to beat her."

"Of course, but he might be interested in asking why. He might even ask her about other things if he gained the impression you were trying to frighten her into silence. Of course, a slave's testimony isn't worth much, but once an investigation begins, others may come forward. Even if you're innocent, it could be awkward."

I had spoken quietly, but he knew exactly what I meant, and he swallowed and looked ill at ease. It took no great intelligence to guess the reason. Situated as he was, the inn would be the natural meeting place of the thieves who haunted the river. Stolen property changed hands, to be stored and later sent down the river to the coast. Forgers, tax-evaders, wanted criminals seeking passage—all would be potential sources of income to an unscrupulous man.

"Of course," I added casually, "the girl could always be sold to some passing stranger who would carry her well away from here."

"Who would want to buy a bitch like that?" His eyes widened as he looked at me, then narrowed. "You?"

"I might be interested if the price was right. The amphitheater can always use girls to entertain the crowd. Give her a knife and set her to face a dozen wild dogs—" I broke off, shrugging. "How much?"

"She's yours for five gold pieces."

I laughed. "For that? I'll give you three." He took it and the girl was mine.

CHAPTER NINE

Her name was Lavinia Viventia. Bathed and dressed in clean garments, her hair washed and wound in a crest, she looked like the daughter of nobility she claimed to be. I was willing to believe her. Every member of the Iceni who owned land and a chariot was a noble and allowed by tribal custom to sit in Council. Her Latin was good which, coupled with her ability to read and write, gave credence to her claim.

On our journey down the Rhone I leaned back against the bales with which the barge was loaded and studied her. She was, I guessed, about nineteen, and even though starved, her body showed the swelling contours of femininity. Her face was oval, her lips full, her eyes huge beneath the upward slant of her brows. Her chin was round and firm with a cleft. She was a beauty, and with good food and rest her attractiveness would grow.

Meeting my eyes she said, in Iceni, "Atilus, are you going to sell me to the arena?"

"No. When we reach Lyons I'll arrange for you to be free."

"But why? Romans aren't generous. Why should

you buy me to set me free?"

"I'm not a Roman," I said patiently. "I've told you that. I am of the Iceni just as you are. Perhaps that's why I bought you."

"To set me free? But what will I do then?" She came to sit beside me, looking small and helpless and more than a little forlorn. "Why can't I stay with you? I can cook and clean and take care of things while you're busy. I'd be useful in lots of ways."

I sighed, remembering Agonestes's warning when I told him what I'd done.

"She'll be trouble, Atilus. You best let me sell her and have done with it. A gladiator has no time for pity and a lanista even less." He'd shrugged when I'd refused his offer. "Well, don't say that I didn't warn you."

That had been days ago when we'd first started down-river. Now I looked to where he stood on a pile of leveled bales. We'd brought practice equipment with us, and he was facing one of the Thracians. The limited area made it hard to dodge and the man was in trouble. As he went down beneath the net I rose and moved toward him.

"That was bad, Terlius. You were too intent on the trident and forgot to watch the net. Use your shield to block it, and don't forget to cut."

"If I had, master, he would have got me."

"Not if you'd gotten in close. A trident's hard to handle, and you could have taken the thrust on your helmet."

"But—"

"Listen! Sometimes you have to take a wound, but when you do, make sure it's to your advantage. Once the tines are in, it's your chance to attack. Don't worry about getting hurt; no gladiator can avoid that. But take the tines where they don't cripple you or cause a fatal wound." I picked up a sword and shield and donned a helmet. "Polybius, show me how you can handle that net."

Agonestes gave it to him together with the trident. The man was sweating and seemed nervous. He grunted as I attacked, slamming the flat of my sword hard against his flank, swinging it back hard against his arm. Blows that stung but did no damage. After the third exchange I lowered the sword.

"What's the matter with you, Polybius?"

"Master, you're too good for me. No one can beat you."

"Fool!" Anger made my voice harsh. "Think that and you're dead. No one is too good in the arena. Every man can be beaten. No matter who you face, you go in to kill. To kill, you understand? To kill! Kill! Kill!"

"Master!"

"Fight, curse you! Fight!"

I kept him at it for a couple of hours, then took a swim and had the slaves follow the barge along the bank. At night we halted to eat and sleep; during the day I kept them hard at exercise.

CHAPTER TEN

We traveled on to Lyons, then dropped down the Rhone, calling at Nimes, leaving the river to go on to Arles and then to Marseilles. I'd picked up a half-dozen good men, cheap at the price I'd paid. I'd fought them in the amphitheaters as we went along, losing two, replacing them at Marseilles. The wounds some of the others had taken would have time to heal during the rest of our journey to Rome.

I'd decided to go by sea and had booked passage to Ostia. On our last night in Marseilles, Lavinia came into my room. Her face and body were beginning to fill out, but she still looked a young and inexperienced girl. Now, closing the door behind her and coming toward my bed, she wore an expression I had seen before on other women.

"Atilus?"

"What do you want?" I was brusque with fatigue. I'd spent the evening working on the accounts, setting sums received against those paid out, itemizing expenses. The profits as yet were marginal. The figures would not please my partners.

"To talk," she said. "Why have you been avoiding

me?"

"Have I?"

"Yesterday you wouldn't let me accompany you when you went to the amphitheater. Today you wouldn't let me come with you to the docks. Agonestes is better company than you are."

"Then stay with him."

"No." She gave a small laugh. "He's more interested in Verax than in me. He's odd, isn't he? I've been watching him. He should have been a woman."

"He's a good man. A friend."

"Not a lover?" She sat down beside me. "Have you ever had a man as a lover, Atilus?"

"You ask too many questions."

"Have you?"

Sighing, I rose from the bed. Wine stood on the table and I poured a cup. Through the window I could see the masts of ships, the sea beyond, the waves silvered with moonlight.

Without turning I said, "Lavinia, you're free now. Why don't you make your own way?"

"To where?" I heard a rustle as she moved. "I haven't the money to get to Britain and nothing waits for me there anyway. My family are dead or taken captive. Rome rules where once the Iceni held their own." She added quietly, "Do you really want to send me away?"

"Yes."

"Because of the patricians waiting for you in Rome? The spoiled bitches who long for your caress?"

"Perhaps."

"Do you miss them? Turn and look at me, Atilus. Do you?"

I turned to look at her. The long robe she'd worn now lay in a heap on the floor. She reclined naked on the bed, her skin gleaming with the nacreous sheen of a pearl.

"Well, Atilus?"

I sipped my wine as I studied her, letting my eyes drift from the narrow, high-arched feet to the slender calves, the curves of her thighs, the swell of her hips. Her waist was small, her torso slight, accentuating the fullness of her breasts, which were set high and proud. Bone showed on her shoulders, shadows filling the hollows. The delicate column of her neck was as graceful as any culled from a Grecian temple. Her hair, loose, framed the contours of her piquant face.

She said again, "Well, Atilus?"

"You're a child," I said. "Nothing but a child."

"And you're a fool to think so."

"A strong man could break you like a twig."

"And I could turn a strong man weak. You doubt that? Then come to me, Atilus, and find out."

"A challenge?" I smiled and helped myself to more wine. A breeze from the ocean sent a gust through the window and caused the flame of the lamp to gutter, dancing shadows cavorting against the walls. "Girl, with a woman that is a game I never play."

"No, you play your games in the arena. Fighting, killing, watching men die. What is it like, Atilus? How does it feel to order a man to his death?" Then, as I made no answer, she said, "But I forget, once you too had to stand on the sand. To watch as you killed. Why did you do it? Why?"

Greed, necessity, the only way I knew how to make a living, but there was more to it than that. The shouts of the crowd, the adulation, the heady sweetness of victory—an intoxication far greater than that given by wine. And, too, there was the visible proof of superiority.

"Atilus, will you teach me how to fight?"

"No."

"Why not? Women fight in the arena and I want to be one of them."

"You? A child?"

"A woman," she corrected harshly. "I've fought and I've killed. I've burned houses and listened to the screams of those caught within. I've had a Roman beg for his life and laughed as I took it. Don't you ever dare again to call me a child!"

"I apologize."

"And you will teach me to fight?"

I was wearing my tunic with nothing beneath it; now I stripped and stood naked before her.

"Look!" I touched my scars. "You think getting these was enjoyable? Do you want your body to be so adorned? Steel burns when it strikes and the wounds ache as they mend. Men have been driven mad with pain and begged for death as a lover begs for a caress. Sometimes the hammer is a mercy."

"To a man in pain, perhaps—but what mercy can

be given to a woman who is not loved?" She rose and stood before me, looking directly into my eyes. "Let me be your woman," she said softly. "Take me and use me as a man does his mate."

An invitation I had expected, but now that it came I felt a sudden bitterness, a repulsion I could neither understand nor explain.

"As the price for taking you to Rome?" I saw the hurt come into her eyes, the stiffening of her features, yet some demon drove me on. "Your body in return for passage, is that it?"

"No! Atilus, I—"

"Get dressed," I ordered. "And get out. A woman of the Iceni should have more pride." And then, as she reached the door, I added, "We leave with the morning tide."

The sea and the wind were favorable and we made good progress. The days slipped one into the other as we lazed on the deck watching the blur of the coast as it slipped past. We had brought our own food and shared the galley with the crew. Lavinia prepared our meals: bowls of steaming barley thick with meat, fruit, and bread, together with sausage and puddings made of chopped offal and blood mixed with meal. After an initial coldness she regained her earlier warmth and, while neither of us mentioned her visit to my room, we were friendly again by the time we reached Ostia. A short journey and we were in Rome.

My house had changed. The garden had been cleared to provide room for exercise, and cubicles had been built to accommodate the gladiators, slaves, trainers, and attendant guards. Leaving Agonestes to settle the men we had brought with us, I took Lavinia and went in search of Fabia. She was in the kitchen, her broad face shining with sweat, her nose crinkling as she tasted a spoonful of something she had taken from a pot.

"More salt," she decided. "And more garlic."

The cook, a fat Nubian, was sullen. "I'll ruin it."

"It's tasteless as it is. Now do as I say, you fat bitch. I know how to cook if you don't." Dropping the spoon, she turned and saw me. Her face broke into a smile. "Master! Welcome back!"

I'd promoted her to housekeeper and, aside from the cook, she had other female slaves to prepare the food and to clean the house.

"You're looking well, Fabia. Where's Heraculis?"

"At the amphitheater, master." Her eyes drifted to the girl, openly curious.

"This is Lavinia Viventia, a friend. She'll be staying here for a while. Find her a room, and she could probably do with something to eat."

"The poor little thing looks half-starved." Fabia shook her head in maternal concern, indifferent to the fact they were close in years. Leave her with me and I'll have her as plump as a capon."

"Lavinia?"

"I'll be all right, Atilus. You go about your business." As I left I heard her say, "And now, Fabia, you must tell me if your master has any favorite dishes. If he has, you must teach me how to prepare them and, in return,

I'll show you how we cook in the Iceni fashion."

Joining Agonestes, I inspected the cubicles. Most were empty and showed no sign of recent occupancy.

"We've been busy," he said dryly. "We left two dozen gladiators behind when we left and now there are only four. And all are wounded."

The men had been hand-picked, trained, and skillful. Even with a full program, the turnover was high.

"There'll be others at the amphitheater."

"Six," said Agonestes. "It's just as well we returned when we did."

A sentiment echoed by Heraculis when later we sat in the study.

"Master, I'm glad you're back. We need the men you brought with you. Maraccus has arranged for extra bouts next week, and we'd have had to hire freedmen if it hadn't been for those slaves."

"Maraccus?"

"A lanista employed by Livius Titus Valerius. He came a week after you left. He's good, I'll admit it, but he presses hard."

I had arranged for another lanista to handle the men, an old friend I could trust.

"What happened to Haemus?"

"He died." Heraculis shrugged at my expression. "Don't ask me how. One minute he was sitting drinking his wine, the next he was doubled over vomiting blood. Livius naturally had to be informed. A day later Maraccus arrived and practically took over."

Maraccus was a good man, worth having, and Livius

couldn't be blamed for having replaced the dead man. And the books revealed the wisdom of his choice. A lot of money had been made, but trouble loomed ahead.

At the next meeting of the partnership I gave the others the facts.

"We're not big enough to handle what's been happening. There have been too many fights for the number of gladiators we own."

"We're making money." Livius took a grape and ate it while he held my eyes with his own. "Surely that is the whole purpose of the partnership?"

"Of course."

"Then why do you complain?"

Drusillius said quickly, "Let Atilus explain, Livius. That is why we invited him to join us. His knowledge is a valuable asset and one squandered if ignored."

We had met, as usual, in Aquilia's house and, also as usual, Drusillius strove to maintain the peace. Aquilia, watching my face, said, "What is troubling you, Atilus?"

"Maraccus for one. Was I mistaken to think I had your agreement to run the school with a free hand?"

"No. And?"

"A simple hatter of logic. Each time a pair is matched, one gets killed and the other is often wounded. Sometimes the fallen man is given life, but you can't rely on it, and even coming to an arrangement with the editor only helps a little. A wounded man takes time to heal, and has to be fed and cared for while he recovers. We have several who will not be able to fight again this year. Some of the others have been put into the arena too soon after their previous bouts."

Livius took another grape. "They are slaves," he said casually. "They do as they are ordered."

"You can't order a man to give of his best," I said. "You can only persuade him and hope that he will. When a man fights too often, he loses his edge. He falls a little below prime condition. Only a little, perhaps, but it is enough at times to tip the balance. Even if he wins, the chances are he will be badly wounded." To Drusillius I said, "You can understand that. You've seen enough fights to know it happens."

"True," he admitted. "A man can be pressed only so far."

"But we're making money," said Aquilia. "You can't deny that, Atilus."

"We're making it at the expense of our stock. I bought cheap and we're selling dear—but what happens when we have nothing left to sell? And things haven't been handled right. Gladiators have been lost who should have been nursed along to get larger fees. Maraccus is good, but he lacks imagination. I'm not going to ask what orders he was given or by whom, but I'd like to remind you that I was given a free hand."

"Within limits," said Livius.

"None were specified."

"Be reasonable, Atilus. You can't be in two places at the same time. While you're absent buying gladiators, someone has to handle those left behind. Maraccus is a good man and he knows what to do."

"You mean he takes your orders and pushes on regardless," I said bluntly. "That isn't good enough. I've kept him on so far because he's useful, but if he doesn't recognize that I'm the man in charge, I won't allow him to stay." I looked from one to the other. "Does anyone object?"

I was reassured; they did not.

"Now let's talk about the future. The summer is ending and we can just about last out with the fighters we have if they are used with care. But if we hope to maintain our profits next year, we'll have to buy heavily this winter."

"We could gain a little extra from private fights," said Drusillius. "I could arrange for displays which would cater to those more interested in skill than butchery. Third blood, for example, is always popular with those who like to bet, like to watch, but aren't too happy about paying for corpses."

A good idea and I said so. Whoever caused the third wound would be proclaimed the winner—and none of the wounds need be more than surface skin cuts. And, though the fees would be relatively small, every bit of income would help.

Livius agreed. "Exactly, Atilus, but economy is just as important as income. I've been checking your expenses for the recent trip. Was it necessary to provide the slaves with women and wine?"

"I thought so."

"And that slave girl you bought and later freed?"

"She was bought with my own money."

"Even so, there is the matter of housing, food, and transportation."

"Am I to count every sesterce?" I let anger sound in my voice. "If you don't trust me, then maybe it is time we parted company."

"No need for that." Livius made a casual gesture. "A point, no more, but it gives rise to another. Maraccus has no imagination, you say, and I agree, but he is not a man to be ignored. Money will be needed this winter and it must be found. I think it should be possible for us to arrange something. Surely you have a gladiator who can be spared?" He looked at me, his face bland, but his eyes revealed his meaning. "A man whom the crowd would be eager to back?"

He was a subtle man and I sensed why he had mentioned Lavinia and the expenses, Maraccus too. He was not concerned about a few coins, of that I was certain, and his suggestion contained an implied threat. Cooperate or else. I had hinted that the partnership should be ended; had he done the same?

Had Maraccus been introduced into the school in order to take my place?

Would I, too, double over my wine vomiting blood?

Then I saw Aquilia's eyes and noted Drusillius's expression. They gave me the answer. Livius's suggestion was not a threat, it was simple greed. The profits already won they wanted to keep. The money needed for the winter must come from elsewhere.

"It must be done carefully," I said. "I'll arrange a series of fights to build up the reputations of the best men we have left. When I decide who it will be, I'll let you know."

"Send word to me," said Aquilia. "And let it be soon."

Some things can't be hurried, and yet there was no time to waste. Winter was coming and the season would soon be over. I had limited time and I used every minute—arranging fights, bribing owners to gain easy victories, paying men to stand in the tiers and shout my contenders' names.

I ended with three possibles: a Thracian, a myrmillo, and a retiarius. The Thracian was Terlius, who was still a little raw and not too well favored by the crowd. Galus, the myrmillo, was a hulking brute who fought with brawn and not brain, careless of wounds as long as he could go in for the kill. He was a good man and a valuable fighter whom I'd be reluctant to lose. The retiarius, a sneering Spaniard, was as good in his own way and as valuable. He had a habit of swearing at the crowd and throwing obscene gestures when they were against him—a trait that added to his popularity.

On him, the betting would be high and the take good should he fall. Galus too was a good choice, and as time passed, I weighed them both, still unable to decide.

Maraccus was of little help. He was a tough, scarred veteran of the arena. A man without conscience who, after one rough meeting, had accepted my authority. Now he rasped a hand over his stubbled chin and brooded over the problem.

"Galus will be hard to beat, but the Spaniard is like an eel. The crowd loves a swordsman, but the women will go for a pretty face, and the Spaniard has that. On the other hand, Galus has the kind of body the degenerates go for."

No help—and soon came the time for decision.

It had been a busy day and fatigue clogged both my body and brain. The night was still; only the distant screeching of an owl broke the silence. Outside the moonlight gleamed from the walls and cubicles; the straw-wrapped posts in the exercise ground looked like the stunted bodies of men.

The gladiators and slaves were asleep. Maraccus had left to swill wine in a tavern. Agonestes had lingered at the baths and was now probably with some delectable boy.

Alone I considered the two men: Galus or the Spaniard? The myrmillo or the retiarius? Which?

I wanted to keep both, but one would have to go. The odds would be higher on the Spaniard, but Galus could fall at any time, and to save him might be to waste a golden opportunity.

As I reached for wine I heard the creak of a board.

It came again—the sound of a heavy, cautious tread from somewhere down the passage where Lavinia lay sleeping.

Like a mouse she had slipped into the routine of the house, helping Fabia with the cooking, chattering with Heraculis, taking care of the wounded. I was busy and tended to ignore her, yet always I was conscious of her presence. Now, as the creak came again, I rose and stepped to the door.

Outside the passage was in shadow, the single lamp, which usually illuminated it had been extinguished. Ahead of me I heard the sound of heavy breathing, a grunt, the splinter of yielding wood. A patch of dim luminescence showed in the wall. The outline of a bulky figure was framed in the doorway.

Then Lavinia cried out.

She let out a startled cry, not a scream, but I responded as if a shriek had been torn from her throat. Within seconds I was in the room, reaching at the bulk bending over her bed, my arm drawn back, fist clenched, moving forward as I struck. It was like hitting a wall. My fist met solid flesh and muscle, then an arm rose, swept across my chest, slamming me against the wall.

I shouted as I hit, an alarm answered by a flood of light and a querulous voice as Heraculis, blinking, came into the chamber.

"What's the matter? What's all the noise? What's going on?"

In the light I could see Lavinia, off the bed now, standing with her back against a wall, her hands uplifted, the fingers curved into claws. Naked, she glowed in the lamplight.

"Galus?" Heraculis stepped forward, his voice hardening. "What are you doing here?"

Galus stood before the girl, as naked as she was. Great muscles ridged on back and shoulders. Turning, he blinked at the light and from his mouth came the odor of wine.

"Galus, go to bed immediately," I ordered.

"I—" He swayed, one hand lifting to his cropped skull. My blow had left a patch of redness on his cheek. "I must have lost my way. I—" He swallowed. "Is that you, master? I don't know what I'm doing here."

He'd been intent on rape and I could have killed him because of it. I could still kill him—I had the right. A slave, he had struck his master, and for that I could send him to rot on a cross.

"The guards, master?" Heraculis looked at me. "Shall I summon the guards?"

I shook my head and said, smiling, "Come, Galus, I know how it is. You had a little too much to drink and fell asleep and woke and thought you were in a dream. It's happened to me often enough."

"Has it?" He blinked and lifted one thick arm. "A dream?"

"Of a lovely woman. You'll have one soon. She could even be waiting for you in your bed at this moment. Best get back to it and see. In any case, you need rest."

"A woman?"

"Yes. Hurry or she'll get tired of waiting. Go to sleep and she'll come to you. Hurry now."

He would have been hard to subdue if he had gone berserk. He was huge and could have killed us all. But I'd soothed him and like a docile animal, he let me lead him to his cubicle. I left him, my decision made. Galus would be the one to die.

CHAPTER ELEVEN

Death can come to a gladiator in many ways. A blinding flash of sunlight reflected from a blade, a patch of hidden blood or excreta causing a foot to slip, a sudden cramp, a better opponent, a momentary hesitation, the disfavor of the gods—all these are the natural hazards of the arena. But the one thing no fighter can guard against is the determination of his lanista to see him dead.

I had seen it happen many times.

In Ferentis a myrmillo, popular, heavily-backed, had been drugged with the juice of henbane given to him in wine sweetened with honey. He had died on the sand, eyes glazed, mouth gaping, unaware even at the end of what had been done to him. In Luceria cantharides had been given to a cruppellarius who, crazed by the overdose of potent aphrodisiac, had fallen easy prey to a Thracian despite his protective cuirass. In Capua a retiarius had been dazed with opium and literally hacked to pieces for the benefit of his owner and those who had backed his opponent. Fortunes had been made by the unscrupulous.

Now Galus was to die to insure my fortune.

A little belladonna would do it, enough to distort his vision and make every stroke of his sword a wild guess. I knew how much to give and when it should be given and how to disguise its flavor in the wine. Physicians did more than heal, and a certain Egyptian had been accommodating for the sake of gold. His greed had led him to become well-educated in the art of poisoning. An art my partners had use for: I had no choice but to accommodate them. Yet I wanted Galus dead for more than money. During the night I had lain awake, thinking, imagining what would have happened had I not heard the creak of the board. His hands on Lavinia's body, his great strength overcoming her struggles, his knee opening her thighs, the thrust of his turgid flesh into her belly, filling her womb with his seed.

In the dawn she had come to me and sat beside me as a new day had brightened the sky.

"Why, Atilus?"

"What do you mean?"

"You came to me when I needed you," she explained patiently. "Why should you have bothered? You once made it plain how you felt about me."

"That was a long time ago. I was angry."

"Because I offered you my body?"

"Because you cheapened it. Anyway, we are both of the Iceni."

Her smile was enigmatic. "Is that the only reason?"

"Galus is a slave."

"As you once were."

"He had no right."

"And if it had been someone else? Someone not a slave?" She watched my face, waiting for my answer, and when none came she continued, "Your eyes betray you as they did in Marseilles. Don't you realize my spells have worked? That my prayers to the Goddess have been answered? I wanted you to love me, my darling. To love me as I love you—and last night you proved that you do."

"Spells!" The thought irritated .me. "I've no time for your superstitious nonsense. You are a young girl and alone. Someone has to look after you."

"Is that why you came to my room? To look after me?"

"I heard a noise and went to investigate. That's all."

Her face fell and she sat plucking at the fabric of her gown. Time, as Fabia had promised, had put flesh on her bones and, while she was not as plump as a capon, she was far from the scrawny, half-starved girl I had bought from the innkeeper. The urchin had turned into a beautiful woman.

Without looking up she said, "Atilus, have you ever thought of going back home?"

"To Britain? At times, yes. Why do you ask?"

"I'd like to go back. I'm tired of this constant glare and heat of the sun. At home the forests would be cool now and thick with shade. In the morning there would be mist that turns everything into magic and wisps of gossamer on the shrubs as if ghosts had passed and left fragments of themselves behind. You could hear the deer at night calling to their mates and the bark of foxes. Rabbits would run, halting to run again as you turned away, and we could walk hand in hand beside the river and try to catch otters as they dived. Oh, Atilus, I miss home so much!"

As I had once missed it, lying and crying myself to sleep, a child forced to act the man, to march with bleeding feet over alien roads to a harsh servitude. A slave! The memory brought a sickness that filled my throat with gall.

Wine stood on a table and I splashed it into a goblet, drank, refilled the container, and drank again, tasting nothing but bitterness as I gulped the ruby fluid. Lowering the empty goblet, I looked at the hand holding it, the fingers heavy with rings, the bracelets adorning the flesh of my wrist and arm. A fashion of Rome, as the scars I carried were a product of Rome. I myself had turned into a Roman.

Why did this girl have to revive such uncomfortable memories?

"You've forgotten too much, Atilus," she said quietly, as if reading my mind. "You've been in Rome too long. You say that we are both of the Iceni, but that isn't true. You are a Roman now. You dress like one and act like one and think like one. You think of Rome as your home." And then with sudden pleading she added, "Have you forgotten what Rome did to you? Once you were a slave and you have never lost your chains. You wear them with a willing pride. Rome has won you. Your mother died fighting the people you now serve and my parents did the same. Shall I also spit on their memory?"

"You talk like a fool," I said. "And what do you know of my mother?"

"Slaves talk, Atilus. They know. What you are and what you were is common knowledge. Why haven't you married? Is it because an ordinary woman isn't good enough for you? Are you waiting for some old, decadent patrician bitch to give you her wealth in return for your young, strong body? In Marseilles you told me to have pride. Tell me, Atilus, child of the Iceni—where is yours?"

I turned and saw her face and halted my hand an inch from her cheek. Looking at it I said, "It's an old trick in the arena to goad an opponent to make him lose all caution in a blaze of anger. But it's a trick only an expert should play."

"Strike me if you want to, Atilus."

"No."

"Beat me if it will give you pleasure." She pulled the gown from her shoulders to display the rounded flesh, the swelling mounds of her breasts. "Hurt me, whip me, burn me, but for the love of the gods don't ignore me. I love you, Atilus! I love you!"

She had the way of the women of the Iceni, unhampered by false modesty and pride, equal with their men and as ready to invite a man to be their lover as a man was to chase a girl.

"I love you," she said again. "And you love me. That's why you came to me. That's why you tried to kill Galus and would have killed him had he not left me alone. Why did you do that? Why?"

I said harshly, "Because, you fool, if anything comes out of you I want to have put it there."

"A baby?" She rose to embrace me, her cheek warm against my own, her lips close to my ear. "A child, my darling? Your child?" And then with a sudden, overwhelming demand, "Give me your child!"

A time of passion ending only when it became necessary for me to go to the amphitheater and watch Galus die.

He did it badly, swaying like a blinded bull, shouting as the irons burned him into combat, crying as steel opened his flesh. Sounds born not of fear but of bewilderment as his body failed to respond to the orders of his brain. And when finally he hit the sand, he was sobbing like a child.

Dead, he was only a victim of Rome.

"A clean finish," said Maraccus, rubbing his stubbled chin. He had been the one to accompany the gladiator and the irons had been used at his order. "The crowd liked the way he fought, all those swings and shield thrusts, then the blood." He sucked at his teeth. "A couple of times there I thought he might have won."

"Was that when you gave him the irons?"

"A little encouragement, Atilus."

He stared at me with eyes as expressionless as twin plates of agate, but there had been something in the way he had said the words, which told more than their bare meaning. Livius had given him his place, and Livius would have taken no chances.

I said, "Encouragement to fight or to fall, Maraccus?"

"A gladiator goes in to win."

"And Galus lost." I shrugged, dismissing the matter. "Well, it happens."

Leaving him to take care of the others, I went to the area beyond the Gate of Death where the bodies of the dead had been stacked. Agonestes was with me, and leaving him to bribe the slaves, I searched for the corpse of Galus. Already the harpies had been at work; raw flesh showed where a knife had sliced off his genitals. The organ would be sold to a magician to be dried, pounded, sold as an aid to failing virility, or used in some esoteric rite.

Agonestes swore as he saw what had happened.

"The same should be done to the living filth who arranged it. Galus was superstitious and they struck at his beliefs. Unless a man is whole, he will wander in the shadows crying for an eternity as he searches for his lost parts."

"Do you believe that?"

"No, Atilus, but he did. That's why he kept his lost teeth in a bag slung around his neck. See?" He showed me the small pouch hanging from a cord, still intact despite the thieves, the contents valueless even to them. "What are you looking for?"

"Turn him over and open his cheeks."

Agonestes grunted as he obeyed and drew in his breath as he saw the raw burns which had seared the anus. Others marred the flesh between the thighs. The wounds were barely noticeable as he released the round buttocks.

"Maraccus?"

"Yes."

Agonestes said thoughtfully, "Galus was to fall, I know that, but why should Maraccus take a hand? No trainer in his right mind would burn his man in such a fashion. If the slave who applied the irons should talk, things could get awkward."

That was an understatement and I had to do something to minimize the danger. With a knife I slashed at the dead flesh, cutting deep, removing other parts of his body and obliterating all trace of the burns. The slaves who watched could be silenced with money, and Agonestes wouldn't talk. But still more had to be done.

Livius Titus Valerius lived high on the slopes of the Esquiline, his house commanding a wide view of the city. A slave ushered me into the atrium and served wine together with a dish of small cakes. Somewhere music was being played and a woman's soft laughter followed the deeper tones of a man.

I waited, sipping the wine but not touching the cakes. After draining the goblet, I walked about the room, glancing at the rich furnishings and elaborate mosaics and then, losing patience, made my way into the inner courtyard. The musician, an elderly man with a mane of silvery hair, ceased playing when he saw me. A tall, broad-shouldered man stepped toward me, glowering, halting at his master's command.

"Hold, Silius!"

The voice had come from behind a curtain of vines,

but the tone was unmistakable. It was the one a man would use to snap an order to a dog. Like a brand it identified the man who had spoken.

Livius sat on a low couch set before a table loaded with wine and plates of delicacies. The girl I had heard was at his side, a young thing with a pretty, vacuous face and hair far too elaborately dressed for her age. Her clothing was disarranged and she was more than a little drunk.

"Livius!" she said. "You have a guest. A nice guest. You will—" She blinked. "You will introduce us?"

"Meet Atilus—a lanista."

The way he said it was an insult, but one I chose to ignore. The girl was probably the daughter of some rich family who found it amusing to dabble in decadence, and Livius was showing her the way. Not, I guessed, that she needed much showing; within a few years she would be prominent among the creatures who haunted the arenas, bribing gladiators to come to their beds when smeared with the sweat and blood and stench of their victory. Later, if she followed the pattern, she would probably give money to bestiarii to help her couple with beasts.

Some of my thoughts must have showed on my face, for she abruptly straightened and thinned her lips.

"It seems your friend doesn't like me, Livius. I had better leave."

"There is no need." He glared at me as he rested one hand on her thigh. "We shall soon be alone."

"I came to see you, Livius," I said.

"And found it impossible to wait?" He glanced to where his slave, an ex-gladiator now acting as servant and bodyguard, stood waiting. "You are fortunate I kept Silius from you."

I said patiently, "This is a partnership matter and it is urgent."

"For you, perhaps, but not for me. It can wait until later. Be at the usual place at the end of the third watch."

He used the haughty tone of a patrician and gestured to the musician to resume playing. His arrogance was born of his belief in his own superiority and the knowledge of the power and prestige his wealth commanded. Because of this, the woman lounging at his side was willing to have him use her as a plaything. Because of this, Silius, at a word, would willingly kill me.

Perhaps he could do it, but I had my doubts. He was young, hard, and well-built, and he had fought on the sand, but I too had my strength and some experience. Yet the incident firmed my resolve.

I bowed, remembering old warnings to mask anger with a smile. I had done so many times before, to my advantage. In the arena, to act a deceptive part was to set the stage for final victory.

"The others?"

"Will be notified." Again the haughty gesture. "You may go."

Lavinia was waiting when I returned to the house. She looked into my eyes, her own eyes solemn. "Something is troubling you, my darling. Galus?"

"Is dead."

"And the manner of his death?"

"Does it matter?" I looked beyond her to the ravaged garden where the gladiators were resting or nursing their wounds. "Where's Maraccus?"

"He has not yet returned. I think he is celebrating in a tavern somewhere. Agonestes brought the men back." Her hand closed on my arm. "Atilus, take me to your bedchamber."

"Now?"

"Why not?" The pressure of her hand relayed an ancient message. "Remember what you are, my darling, a warrior of the Iceni. Such men do not need to bathe before taking their women. The blood they shed, the smell of it, the sweat on their bodies—all make for fine, strong ones. A true woman is stimulated by the natural scents of her man—only these weak Romans need the stench of perfumes and sweet oils as an accompaniment to their coupling."

I remembered staid matrons who had paid me extra not to bathe before coming to them after a combat, who reveled in the stains and stinks of victory. But I said nothing. Instead I guided her to my room and was met with a surprise as I passed through the door.

The place had been converted.

A curtain blocked the, window and the sunlight beyond so that the room was filled with a soft, eerie gloom. On all sides branches had been placed, covering the walls with their leaves. The room looked like a forest glade. Only the bed was untouched, and the table set at its foot, on which rested a bowl half-filled with liquid. I knew what it was, what it had to be—a mixture of wine and salt—the ceremonial wedding drink. The room had been turned into a ceremonial bower.

"The marriage rites of the Iceni," said Lavinia softly. "Surely you remember? We have no Druid to bless the union or relatives to act as witnesses, but they are unimportant. Drink, Atilus. Share the salted wine and say the words that will make us one. Marry me, my darling. Marry me!"

Here and now by the simple rites of my people, later by the customs of Rome, we would be married. The child I strove to plant in her belly would not grow to become a fatherless waif.

"Darling!" She squirmed beneath me, her naked flesh hot against my own, consumed by the passion that had hardened her nipples and drenched the interior of her thighs. "Darling! My darling! My man! My husband! My life!"

My woman! My companion! My wife!

I held her to me in possessive desire, cradling her as the fires eased, feeling the tenderness, the concern of a man lost and helpless without the thing he holds most precious. On the sand it could be a sword, a shield, a lucky charm. Here in the small arena of the bed it was Lavinia, who looked as my mother must have looked when she was young. Lavinia, who had the same spirit, the same, unselfish willingness to surrender, to please. She wakened in me the fires that are the gift of the gods to men. What greater pleasure can a woman give?

"Darling?" She grumbled as I moved, snuggling close, her arms wrapped around me, her cheek against my chest, the rich mane of her hair a curtain to grace our nakedness. "Don't move, darling. Stay as you are."

"I must leave."

"On our wedding night?" She lifted herself to look down into my face and my eyes followed the enticing movement of her breasts. Like the rest of her they were dewed with perspiration. "Atilus, you can't!"

"I must." Gently I disengaged myself, skin stuck to skin, parting with reluctance. "A matter of business. There are things I have to settle."

"Galus?"

"He's dead. Forget him." I lifted a lock of hair from her lips and kissed them. "I'm concerned with the living, with you, my darling, and what you could be carrying." My hand gently stroked the soft contours of her belly. It was almost as flat as my own, but already, in imagination, I could feel the drum-taut roundness, the kick of impatient life. "Arrangements must be made and time is getting short for my appointment. I need to bathe and dress and—" I pushed away her questing hands. "Behave yourself, woman! Your man goes to war!"

I said it as a joke, but it wasn't far from the truth. There would be struggle and a conflict of interests and argument, but I had already decided how it would end. As the first watch drew to a close I made my way through the streets to the house of Aquilia Sabina. On the way Silius tried to kill me.

CHAPTER TWELVE

He made his attack as I turned a corner. The junction was illuminated by a torch held by a bronze ring. A fitful gust of wind caused the fire to flare and throw dancing shadows over the blank walls and shuttered windows of the facing houses. I heard the rasp of a sandal, saw a shadow larger than the others, and had turned to meet him before he could reach me.

He was a fool, a man accustomed to dominating others by his size and aggression. He was a slave aping his master and too confident for his own good. He had forgotten my prowess in the arena.

The dagger in his hand was held like a sword, thumb to the blade, the point sweeping upward in a vicious blow to my stomach, which would have ripped it open and spilled my guts had it landed as he had intended. But it missed, and Silius staggered as the force of his momentum carried him forward.

"Drop it, you fool!" I snapped my anger. "Drop it!"

He blinked, not yet realizing that my spring to one side had been no accident. As he advanced again, I tensed, poised, my hands extended a little, the fingers held close and the thumbs held upright. It was a posture

I had seen small men from the East adopt at a private display of wrestling during which they had shown that even a big man could be brought down by one of their size. A matter of delicate points, one had explained afterward.

This time Silius was more cautious. As he came in he feinted, weaved a little to his left, reversed the sway as he struck, to veer to the left again as I dodged. The blade hit my tunic, ripping at the fabric and almost touching the skin as I drove my right thumb into his left eye.

I felt it give; the eyeball turned beneath my thrust, and a sudden gush of blood stained my hand as it left its socket to hang like a bruised and oozing grape on his cheek.

A normal man would have screamed and staggered back, his hands flying to shield the injury. Even a gladiator would have grunted beneath the sudden, shocking pain, but the only sound that came from Silius was an animal-like mewing. But I had him. As he recoiled I was on him, my left hand grabbing his knife wrist, the weapon falling as I twisted, feeling bone snap beneath the corded muscle. As the dagger hit the cobbles I jerked up my knee, felt it hit his groin, pushed him away as he doubled, and snatching up the dagger, slipped it neatly between his ribs and into his heart.

As he fell I saw his mouth, open, gaping, tongueless.

"Ho there!" The Watch, always late, had arrived after the affair was over. "Hold! Stand until we reach you!"

It was a stupid instruction and only a stupid man would obey it. The guttering light was behind me; they couldn't have clearly seen my face, and they were far enough away from me to make escape a simple matter of speed. I ran, reached a corner, and bumped into a fat man who went down screaming he was being robbed. Two more corners and a woman called softly from a shadowed alley. She was a prostitute, her voice far more enticing than the goods she offered, but I threw her a coin.

"You've seen nothing. Understand?"

"Yes, Domine, but if you are interested I have a young brother who...."

The rest of the offer was lost as I ran on.

When I arrived at the meeting, Aquilia stared at me, at the blood on my hand and wrist; then, without comment, she arranged for me to wash. My tunic, aside from the rip, was unmarked, but the blade that had torn the cloth could have taken my life, and I was in no gentle frame of mind when I joined the others. Drusillius looked at me from where he lounged on his couch and Livius, after a sharp glance, resumed his normal, languid pose.

As Aquilia handed us wine I said, "One question, Livius."

"Only one?" He controlled himself well.

"What is the question, Atilus?" Drusillius was curious. So was Aquilia.

I said bluntly, "I want the truth. Did you give orders for Maraccus to take a hand in putting Galus down?"

"I? No," said Drusillius. "Is that what you want to ask Livius?"

"Yes, and I want an answer."

"Which I see no reason to give." Livius toyed with a pomegranate. "I think you forget yourself, Atilus."

"And you forget why we are assembled here. We are partners, remember? I'm no slave crawling at the feet of patricians. Your airs and graces don't impress me, Livius, you came to me and asked me to join you. I did. We have all made money. Apparently you thought we could make more. Why did you tell Maraccus to see that Galus fell? Didn't you trust me?"

"A man can change," he said coldly. "And too much was at stake to take needless chances. If you had suffered a fit of remorse, for example, all of us would have lost. It seemed wise to take certain steps. Maraccus, I know, has no qualms about how he earns his gold."

"No qualms and no brains," I snapped. "A fault repeated by yourself."

"How, Atilus?" Aquilia cut in. "Livius may have been wrong to go above your head, but what harm did he do?"

I drank wine before answering. It eased my throat and gave me time to cool. Anger was of no use when dealing with ignorance.

"You're aware of the arena," I said. "You visit it, you use it, you do your best to manipulate it, but you don't *know* it. Isn't that why you made me your partner? Didn't you need my skill and experience and knowledge of how things are done? Maraccus is a blunt, stupid fool too often in the taverns, where he drinks too much wine. Such a man will talk. He will boast and show his gold and promise he will get more. Harpies will act as his sycophants and, before you know it, he will be working for them and not you. He won't realize it, of course, but that's what will happen. But that isn't all. You told him to see that Galus fell—do you know how he did it? Not as I did, with a little something put into his wine. Not as it should be done by a careful use of subtle means which leave no trace. No, the fool burned his private parts with hot irons. He seared his anus—can you even begin to guess what that could do to a fighter trying to concentrate?"

"Does it matter as long as he falls?"

"It matters." I glared at Livius, wishing that it had been his eye I had gouged from its socket, his body I had left lying in the narrow street. "People are watching: other gladiators, their owners, those who wagered money on the outcome. The editor, the crowd, the Master of Games. Do you take them for fools? Once the suspicion is aroused that a lanista is arranging for his fighters to go down, his credit is lost forever. He won't be able to arrange fights and no free gladiator will work with him. He could even end up knifed in some dark alley." I stared hard at Livius. "It's my repu-tation at stake here. One I've built over a dozen years, and I'm not having it thrown away. Maraccus could talk, or the slave who applied the hot irons at his direc-tion, or even the man who collected a certain organ from the body. Anyone could have spotted the burns and remarked on them and passed the word. That can't happen now, but I can't rely on something similar not happening again. That's why I'm leaving the partnership."

Aquilia said sharply, "Atilus! You don't mean that!"

"You can't leave." Drusillius was more practical. "We have an agreement."

"Which has been broken. I was promised a free hand and there has been interference. Livius provided it. You can also thank him for having made up my mind to break the contract. I went to see him, but his attitude convinced me that he considered me no longer necessary to the partnership. So I want an immediate examination and audit of the books and all assets."

There was some argument, but not as much as I had expected. Livius would continue with Maraccus, but Drusillius wanted no part of the arrangement and hinted, as he followed the other into the night, that a new opportunity might shortly be coming my way.

Aquilia shrugged when I mentioned it.

"He is an odd man at times, Atilus, and has some strange ideas. He might want you to join a trading venture to the unknown islands that lie beyond Britain, or found a new city in Africa. Most likely he could be getting interested in laying the groundwork for establishing amphitheaters in Greece. They will come, and the one who gets in early could make a fortune." She patted the couch at her side. "Now sit and drink some wine and tell me all about that dark-haired beauty you've become so enamored of."

We were alone—not even a slave was in attendance—and next to me I could feel the warm heat of her thigh. From outside came the rumble of carts, unnaturally loud as they echoed through the night.

"Noise." Aquilia shook her head. "How I am beginning to hate it."

"What do you know of Lavinia?"

"Atilus! Don't look at me like that!" Smiling, she patted my hands. "There are no secrets in Rome, surely you know that? Gossip is carried by slaves and your young barbarian has aroused interest. More than one patrician would be glad to take your place. You are lovers, of course?"

"Yes."

"As always, you are honest. A lesser man would have lied and so insulted my intelligence. Of course you are lovers." Her hands pressed mine with a sudden urgency. "But does that mean I now have no place in your life?"

"Of course not."

"You are good to say so. And the future?" She sighed as I told her. "Marriage. How I envy her. We resemble each other a little, or so I have been told. Is it so?"

"You could be taken for sisters."

"In a bad light and only by those with poor eyes." She smiled as I shook my head. "Don't flatter me, my darling."

"I don't have to do that, Aquilia. You are lovely and you know it."

"And, Atilus, always you know how to treat a woman." Again her hands pressed mine; then, as if by an effort of will, she released them and straightened. "That blood on your hand—did Livius put it there?"

"I am sure of it. It came from his slave."

"And you said nothing. He could try again, Atilus."

"For what reason?"

"It could have been that you merely stood in his way, and killing you would have both cleared the field and added more to his share of the profits. Have you seen his new paramour?"

"Yes, a child."

"You are being kind. She is vile and you know it, and that very vileness seems to attract Livius. Once it was not so, but then Rome was strong and held certain things to be virtues. Now, only money is important and the ancient standards are mocked. But don't underestimate Livius—to please his new toy he would set you to be tortured to death while she watched. It would be best for you to stay out of sight for a while. Leave Rome, as I intend to do."

"Leave Rome? You?"

"I am tired of it. The stinks, the noise, and above all, this intolerable heat. Will the summer never end? There is talk of disease breaking out in the hovels along the Tiber, and it is impossible to go out and remain free of dust. I have a villa on the coast near Syracuse. The wind blows from the sea and fountains cool even those fresh breezes. Come with me and bring your friend."

"Lavinia?"

"The Greek. I am not fool enough to introduce such competition in my household. The nights can be long in Sicily and a woman needs her comforts. Agonestes will be an asset; there are those who would be willing to make him welcome." Then, more softly, she said, "Come with me, my darling. For a few weeks at the most. Surely your new love will not begrudge me that little happiness?"

"More than begrudge," I said. "The Iceni may be under the domination of Rome, but they still have their pride. Lavinia would follow us with a knife and, when she found us, she would use it."

"As would I at her age. As would any woman who truly loved her man. Well, do one thing for me at least."

"Such as?"

"Escort me to Ostia."

"With Agonestes?" I smiled at her expression. "We should be chaperoned, Aquilia—remember Lavinia and her knife."

CHAPTER THIRTEEN

From Rome to Ostia is a journey of fourteen miles, which we covered in slow, easy stages. Aquilia was carried in a litter, Agonestes and I rode horses. The road was busy with couriers galloping past and the lumbering carts and the occasional chariot that sent pedestrians diving into the ditches for safety. We reached the seaport in the early afternoon and, diplomatically leaving Agonestes to settle the woman in an inn and arrange for her passage to Sicily, I went to have a look at the market where merchants of a dozen lands plied their trade.

"Atilus!" Gallus Caecina's roar rose above the babble of those eager to gain my attention. "By the gods, what are you doing in Ostia?"

"What are you?" I gripped his shoulders and smiled at my old teacher. The years had been kind to him; his face had filled a little and he had gained weight and his eyes sparkled with a new clarity. "You're looking well. Retirement suits you."

"Work, you mean. Up at dawn and out in the fields until dusk. But you're right, the change from the school did me good. As you were right about where I should go. Pompeii is the place for me. I've a good farm and a villa overlooking the sea. All the room I could use to accommodate friends, and all the food and wine they can consume."

"You got it cheap, eh?"

"Cheap enough. As you said, the earthquakes had frightened the owners and they wanted to sell. And with the amphitheater closed there isn't much life. But why are we standing here? Let's find a tavern and order wine and you can tell me all that's been happening."

He blinked when I told him of Lavinia.

"So you've finally been hooked! She must be quite a girl!"

"She is."

"Then look after her. It isn't often a man finds the matching piece of his heart, and when he does, he is favored by the gods. When are you going to bring her to visit me?" Then, as I hesitated, he said, "Come for Saturnalia. You'd enjoy it and I could do with some help."

That I doubted. The festival when slaves adopted the clothes and mannerisms of their masters was a time of wild nonsense usually ending in a wanton orgy, but I couldn't imagine a thing Gallus needed help to handle. He looked abashed when I told him so.

"All right, Atilus, I can manage, but it's a big villa and I get a little lonely at such times. And, to be honest, you were right about one thing. I miss talk of the arena. The young men are good enough in their way, but few of them have actually seen a complete munera. I've to explain too much. Come down and let us drink and eat and fight old games again. Yes?"

"You're tempting me, Gallus. But Saturnalia's months away yet."

"Less than three. You'll think about it?" He smiled as I nodded and changed the subject. "You should have been here last week. Nero took ship to Antium and made it a real occasion. Silly, really—the place is only down the coast—but he set out as if he intended to conquer another Britain. Biremes, lighters, merchantmen, even a trireme, all with pennants flying and marines standing in position. I'll bet those rowers sweated before they dropped him off. Still, it made a show. One of the biremes came from Ravenna bearing dispatches and had a little fun off Tarentum. You'll see what I mean if you come to see me off."

"When?"

"Within the hour. A coaster is giving me passage as far as Cumae, and I can hire carriers there."

He left, waving, making me promise again to visit him at the end of the year. It was a promise I might keep; after the sultry heat of Rome, the sea air would do Lavinia good, and now that I'd ended my participation in the partnership there was nothing to keep me in the city.

The mystery he'd mentioned was the justice meted out to those captured in the action off Tarentum.

I paused before a line of them suspended on crosses facing out to sea. They were a dirty, degenerate bunch, made no better by their wounds. Their blood-soaked rags were grimed and thick with flies. More flies crawled over faces and eyes, feasting on the orbs of those who had died, rising in a cloud from those of the living when, weakly, they jerked their heads.

The dead were the lucky ones. The living, parched, tormented by cramps, writhed on the crosses, lifting their weight on the blocks nailed beneath their feet in order to ease the constriction of their chests.

"We're breaking their legs at dusk," said a legionary who stood on guard. "Those still living, that is. If you want to see a little fun, come along then. Some of them start praying and others start cursing, especially when the rubbish begins to fly." He yelled at a group of youngsters who had thrown dung at the crucified men. "Get away from here! That dirt can hit others! Get away, you young demons!" Shrugging, he turned to me, leaning on his spear. "You can't blame them. Some of them are orphans because of scum like this."

"Pirates?"

"Wolves of the sea." He spat contemptuously. "To me they're vermin. Many an honest man has gasped out his breath because of them. Well, hanging up there, they can think about that. And maybe they'll warn others not to follow the same vile trade."

Aquilia left an hour later, weeping as she made her farewells, her tears directed more toward me than toward her leaving Rome.

"You'll come to see me, Atilus?"

"I'll try."

"No," she said. "You won't come. Instead you'll be

making that girl of yours the happiest woman in the world. By the gods, how I envy her!"

"Aquilia! I shall think of you!"

"Yes," she said. "Think of me at times. Remember what we shared and enjoyed. At least give me that. And remember, darling, you are welcome at any time. You, your friend and, yes, your new love. Perhaps she will be kind enough to share her happiness with an old, stupid woman."

One step and I was close to her, her body enfolded in my arms.

"Not old," I said. "Never stupid, and certainly not unloved. Now smile. Tears at the start of a journey are a bad omen. Smile, darling. Smile. The world is not ending."

For a moment she stared at me, then her arms closed around my neck and her lips, warm and hungry, found my own. For a while we stood like two young lovers and then, abruptly, she had left me and was on the ship and hurrying toward her cabin.

Agonestes joined me as the thud of the hortator's mallet, beating time for the rowers, echoed over the widening gap between the galley and the wharf.

"A good woman, Atilus, and a good friend. She loves you in her fashion."

And loved me more, perhaps, because I did not cling and, like a leech, suck her bounty.

"A friend," I said. "One I would like to keep. Well, Agonestes, let's get back to Rome."

"Now?"

"Why not?"

"It's getting dark," he explained. "The roads will be cluttered with carts. Mounts will be hard to come by; and we'll arrive tired." He added weakly, "And I've met someone whom I'd like to know better. One night, Atilus, where's the harm?"

CHAPTER FOURTEEN

The next morning we left for Rome. As we approached smoke was visible far down the road, and I cursed the flying chariots and mounted couriers who blocked the way. But the true picture didn't become apparent until, from the brow of a hill, I looked down at the city.

"By the gods!" Agonestes, at my side, voiced his horror. "Rome is burning! It's a sea of flame!"

An ocean that roared with a sound like waves driven by a wind. One which threw leaping streamers of flame high into the air, each burning column attended by a host of sparks which swirled and spun as if in a drunken ecstasy. Ash rose from the holocaust to drift and fall like sooted rain. A breeze, driven by heat from the city, carried a stench of charred meat, burning blood, sizzling fat, and seared hair.

"Subura," said Agonestes. He sounded ill. "Have the gods no love for their worshippers? The tenements are burning!"

Subura was made up of tenements, each with a multitude of floors, each cubicle holding its load of human flesh. Men, women, and children were trapped now by the flames that ate at the stairs and roared up the open spaces. Babies were screaming beneath the touch of flame, roasting, their odors joining the rest. Without water the fires couldn't be stopped and water was available only at the public fountains. And they, like the slums of Rome, were wreathed in fire.

"Atilus!" Agonestes tried to halt me as I drove my heels into the sides of my horse. "Wait! You can't—"

"Esquiline is burning and Lavinia is in the house." I tore my arm from his hand. "Lavinia, you understand? I've got to find her."

"Not that way." He guided his horse against mine, sending it from the road. "We'll go to the other side of the city. The Colline Gate. It's clearer around there."

"No!" It would take too long and I was too impatient. "Let me go, Agonestes!"

My horse made the decision. Frightened by the noise, the crowds, and the scent of burning, it suddenly reared and bolted down the hill, back toward the road. A man yelled as, hit by the beast's shoulder, he spun and fell, a litter of pans falling with him, their clatter adding to the animal's terror. Again it reared and this time I was thrown, landing heavily to roll beneath running feet, to rise soiled and with blood trickling from a minor wound on my temple.

Agonestes was nowhere to be seen and I wasted no time looking for him. Instead I fought my way through the crowd, using elbows, knees, and fists when I had to in order to make progress. At the gate a legionary tried to stop me.

"Halt! No admittance to the city!"

"Out of my way, fool!"

"You can't pass through. Orders of the Senate." His voice was brusque. "We need room for those concerned with fire prevention and safety."

He fell aside as I threw my weight against his shield, and without looking back, I passed into the city and thrust my way through the narrow streets.

The place was an inferno, the air thick with drifting ash, sharp explosions coming from burning trees as they split to send more sparks rising upward and outward. Some fell on me, burning holes in my tunic before I could pass through a belt of flames into a relatively quiet spot, which the fire hadn't yet reached.

The progress of the flames was erratic, and governed by wind and terrain. In one area there was a measure of calm. Shopkeepers were closing and barring their premises, more concerned about the prospect of looting than the threat of destruction by fire. Armed patrols moved from house to house, forcing the occupants to evacuate their homes. From all sides came the horns and whistles of the fire brigades as they worked in their various sectors.

"Stand back!" An officer, his face smeared with soot, his eyes red from smoke, waved at me as I approached a crossing. "Stay where you are!" Running toward me, he caught my arm. "The house is about to fall, you fool! Do you want to be buried? We're clearing an area to halt the fire."

The house crashed as he spoke, dust billowing

from shattered plaster, wood splintering and shards of marble and stone littering the street. Others followed as sweating guards directed slaves who were tearing at the walls, adding their own strength, turning a neat line of homes into rubble.

"It's the only way," said the officer. "We've got to make a gap the fire can't cross."

"How did it start?"

"At the Circus. One of the sellers of cakes or something must have spilt some oil on a stove and the flames got out of hand. You know how dry it's been. The partitions must have been like tinder, and before anyone could do anything about it, the entire row of booths was blazing."

The Circus Maximus had been surrounded by small shops filled with oil, candles, waxen images of the gods, perfumes, fabrics, a host of combustible items all dried by the summer heat.

"We might have contained it if it hadn't been for the wind," continued the officer. "As the shops burned, a breeze sprang up and carried sparks over the city. Some places were unlucky. They caught and created updrafts and whirlpools of flame. Since then it's been a nonstop battle."

He swore as, running toward him, a man screamed, "My house! You barbarians! By what right do you destroy my property?"

"The order of the Senate."

"Liar!"

"The Emperor, then, if it makes you feel any better."

The officer scowled. As the wailing man lunged to search the ruins for items of value, he said with disgust, "That's all they think about. Rome is burning and they worry about the household lares and the death masks of their ancestors. They should be in Subura. The poor bastards are roasting in the thousands."

Their screams accompanied me as I raced toward Esquiline. The smoke thickened as I reached the lower slopes of the hill, the red glow of flame spurting from a building higher up as though it were blood gushing from a new-made wound. Scorched, my tunic burned, face and hands thick with soot, I gave thanks to the gods as I saw my house. It was still standing, but wreathed with flame from the burning garden, the roof, the flaming outhouses.

"Lavinia!" I shouted as I ran. "Lavinia!"

In the smoke something moved. A man, his hands loaded with things of value, small items that he dropped as he saw me and snatched out a knife. He was a looter and one ready to kill to save himself from the cross he had already earned.

He lunged and I felt the burn of steel touch my side as I darted to one side, snatching up a length of burning timber, thrusting it into his face as, again, he attacked. The knife fell as he screamed, lifting hands to his ruined face, his blinded eyes. Leaving him to stagger in the debris, lost in a burning darkness, I ran into the house.

"Lavinia!"

A rustle and crash to one side.

"Lavinia!"

The house was empty. A dead slave lay with his throat cut, another was doubled over in a pool of blood. From somewhere close a wall collapsed and fire rose in a red curtain as it fed on the ruins. In a few minutes the place would be a raging inferno in which nothing could remain alive.

"Lavinia!" I shouted for the last time. "Lavinia, my darling! Lavinia!"

Above the hungry rustle of the flames I heard a cry, a low moaning.

"Help me! Master, help me!"

Heat had cracked the walls of the study and a falling wall had sent a beam crashing through the shelves that held the scrolls and records. Beneath it I saw a slight, crumpled figure, a wizened, agonized face.

"Heraculis!"

"Master! My legs—I can't move them!"

The beam had trapped them against the floor. Stooping, I gripped hold, strained, lifted the massive weight a little.

"Move!"

"I can't." Heraculis sucked in his breath. "A little more!"

Blood thundered in my ears as I. heaved at the beam, legs straddled and set hard against the floor while my back and shoulders did their work. The timber moved, halted, rose a little.

"Now! Hurry!"

I heard a rustle, a slither, then a weak voice.

"I'm free, master."

The timber fell with a crash as I released it. "Where's Lavinia?"

"She's safe, master. I sent her to Mars Field with the others. Fabia is attending her and some of the gladiators are fit enough to act as escort."

"And?"

"I wanted to save the accounts and whatever else I could manage. I came back. Some looters came and I hid in the study. The wall collapsed and frightened them away, I think. I must have been knocked out because the next thing I remember was hearing you calling." He drew in his breath in pain. "Master, my legs!"

They had been bruised, perhaps even broken, but there was no time to find out. Lifting him, I cradled him in my arms and ran outside. A wall of flame rose before me, the heat singeing the hair on my head. I ran back into the house; looked through a window, and saw more flame. It surrounded us on every side and more was eating at the roof.

"Hold your breath," I said. "Close your eyes and press your face against me."

Jumping from the window with Heraculis in my arms, I plunged into a furnace.

Heat rose all around me, beating at my face, my hands. Hair flared on my head and left ash on my legs and arms. Had I tripped and fallen, we both would have died. As it was the gods were kind, and I broke through into a burned-out area beyond.

"The house, master!" Heraculis was staring past me, his face crinkled as if he was crying. "The beautiful house!"

"Forget it." A house could be replaced. "Let's get to Mars Field."

The place was crowded. Little groups of distraught people were sitting or standing, watching as all they possessed went up in flames. Many were badly hurt and some seemed to have gone insane.

"The Emperor!" A man grabbed at me and babbled as he loped at my side. "Nero did this! He wants to raze the city. I've heard him talk about finding Rome built of mud and leaving it built of marble. He's watching now, playing his lyre."

"Rubbish!"

"It's true! Why else did the soldiers tear down houses and set fires?"

"They had to make gaps to halt the spread of the flames. Some houses were probably burned to do just that. And Nero isn't in the palace. He took ship for Antium days ago."

He wasn't listening. Before I had finished he'd run off, screaming, accosting more strangers with his wild story. If he continued one of them would probably kill him, but I wasn't interested in his fate. How, among all these people, could I find Lavinia?

Agonestes saved me the trouble. He came riding through the crowd to halt at my wave. He stared at me as if seeing a ghost.

"Atilus, is that you?"

"Can't you recognize me?"

"Under that blood and soot and those blisters? Man, you're lucky to be alive!"

He'd ridden around the city, entering by the Colline Gate, and had found Lavinia almost at once. She came running toward me, arms open, her body soft and comforting against my own.

"Darling! Atilus, my darling!"

"Are you well?"

"Yes. Yes, of course, but you?" Her eyes examined me. "And poor Heraculis?"

Fabia was helping him down from the back of the horse, fretting over him as a mother would over her child. To one side, what gladiators and slaves remained loyal formed a tight little group. Heraculis had provided them with food and wine, and I poured a cup down his throat as Fabia covered him with oil.

"Master! My legs?"

"They're bruised, but no bones are broken. They may hurt for a while, but they'll soon be as good as new." Rising, I gestured Fabia to join me out of earshot. "Help him," I said. "When he can walk unaided, I'll give you your freedom."

"You won't send me away!"

"No. You'll just be able to box his ears without risking punishment the next time he runs his hands up your skirts."

I left her with her face wreathed in smiles and joined Lavinia where she stood looking at the flames that gilded the darkening sky. It was later than I'd thought.

Soon it would be night, but when it came, there would be no darkness. The fire would see to that.

"Rome," she said softly. "Once I prayed for the day I'd see it burn."

So had I, but Rome wasn't just a city, and it was impossible to burn a world. And yet, watching the flames eat into the heart of the Empire, I was reminded of another fire and of a woman who had crouched over it before the great battle at Brentwood, when Claudius had taken Britain for his own. Was I now seeing the fruit of her curse?

I turned and thought I saw her, then realized it was Lavinia who stood staring at the holocaust with the gleam of victory in her eyes. Then, as she looked at me in turn, the gleam became that of unshed tears.

"Atilus! Oh, my husband, what are we to do?"

When an egg breaks from the thrust of the life inside, the chick has the choice of a world in which to roam. I had been as much a prisoner as a bird unhatched. The bars that held me had been of gold fashioned by greed, hate, lust for revenge, the love of death dealt on the sand. The arena had cursed me and extracted its price for survival. I had forgotten who and what I was. Now, that golden world shattered, I could see clearly again at last.

"We go home, Lavinia," I said. "Home to where we belong."

To Britain, to the lands of the Iceni, to the misted groves where men were not butchered for a holiday, and where my children could run free.

ABOUT THE AUTHOR

English writer **E. C. TUBB** is internationally known, having been translated into more than a dozen languages. In a sixty-year writing career he published over 120 novels, and more than 200 science fiction short stories in such magazines as *Astounding/Analog*, *Authentic*, *Fantasy Adventures*, *Galaxy*, *Nebula*, *New Worlds*, *Science Fantasy*, and *Vision of Tomorrow*.

Tubb's early science fiction novels were exciting adventure stories, written in the prevailing fashion of the early 1950s. Yet, from his very first novel, his work was characterized at all times by a sense of plausibility, logic, and human insight. These qualities were even more evident in his short stories, which were frequently anthologized.

By 1956 his output included adventure, detective stories, and westerns, but he remained best known for his numerous science fiction novels, of which *Alien Dust* (1955) and *The Space Born* (1956) were acknowledged classics. Tubb became famous for his long-running "Dumarest of Terra" series of novels, the galaxy-spanning saga of Earl Dumarest and his search to find his way back across the stars to the legendary lost planet where he was born—Earth. They eventually spanned thirty-three titles, the final one, *Child of Earth*, appearing in November 2008. Equally well known were his *Space 1999* TV novelizations, and his "Cap Kennedy" novels. Some of his finest SF short stories were collected in *The Best Science Fiction of E. C. Tubb* (Wildside, 2003). Tubb continued to write dynamic science fiction novels right up to his death in October, 2010.

www.ingramcontent.com/pod-product-compliance
Lightning Source LLC
Chambersburg PA
CBHW050743250626
47155CB00005B/1897